THE DEVIL IS A PART-TIMER!

17

SATOSHI WAGAHARA

ILLUSTRATION BY
029 (ONIKU)

MgRonald 6

CONTENTS

The Devil's Boss Rediscovers Her Inexperience

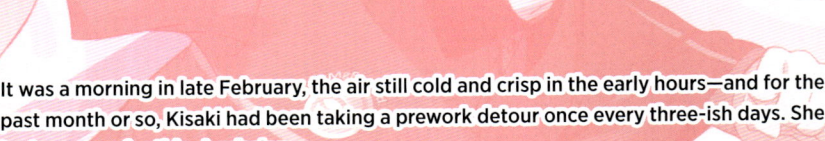

It was a morning in late February, the air still cold and crisp in the early hours—and for the past month or so, Kisaki had been taking a prework detour once every three-ish days. She had a reason for this. A mission.

"Still? They're taking *forever*."

But yet again, today's mission had ended in failure. She pouted at the cup of coffee she had purchased at the adjacent convenience store.

"All this for just a hundred yen... The convenience-store industry must be just as crazy competitive as mine."

To be frank, the coffee was far better than it had any business being, coming from a corner shop at a low, flat price that already included tax. There were cafés all over the city that'd serve up an inferior cup and blithely charge you around five hundred yen for the privilege.

"Maybe consumers are a lot smarter than people give them credit for."

Sipping her hundred-yen coffee, the product of a huge monetary and personnel investment from one gigantic corporation or the other, Kisaki looked back at the place she made it her mission to visit lately. There, next to the convenience store, was an empty retail space that had been listed for sale until a month ago. Still nurturing dreams of going independent and running her own bar-café, Kisaki had taken a tour of the space a while back, more out of curiosity than anything else. When the real estate agent heard what she was looking for, he attempted to woo her by offering the fixtures and such left by the space's previous restaurant tenant at a low cost, which could have potentially saved her a great deal of money.

The space was situated in a relatively new building, in a redeveloping residential neighborhood. Older homes were giving way to shiny new condo buildings, and as the real estate agent put it, Kisaki could expect a steady stream of locals to cater to. The size and monthly rent were both decent for the Sasazuka area of Shibuya ward. But to Kisaki, her senses and instincts honed by years of working for a large chain, something felt off. If the conditions were *this* good, there must be something sinister lurking under the surface—and after making her second visit to check out her hunch, she crossed the space off her mental checklist.

In which case, why not install a place that didn't need customers physically visiting it? With the right staff, a pizza joint doing most of its business by delivery could have the entire neighborhood as a customer base. If the area was home to lots of single people, many of them might be in the market for a part-time job. Moreover, setting up in a location that wasn't a hot spot meant the business could save on rent. Dombino also offered a free pizza if you ordered at least two and came to pick them up, a killer deal that had become a hit for them. Turned out that many people who lived nearby one of their stores were willing to suffer a little bit of inconvenience for a free pie.

Really, it was the ideal tenant for a rental space like this.

"This makes me nervous."

"What's wrong? If you like, you can always talk about it with me..."

"Talking with *you* would just make me more nervous. Shut up."

"Absolutely!"

Sarue was an annoyance, but at least he followed her instructions.

Ignoring him for the moment, Kisaki thought things over. *How could I be so narrow-minded? Can I really do something as big as going independent when I'm like this?*

No matter how long she had been managing a dining establishment, her skills were still oriented toward handling the MgRonald platform, a system perfected over years of operation and expansion. Did she have the skills to build a business from scratch? And what were those skills, exactly? She didn't know.

Still peeved at the smiling man next to her, Kisaki walked on. She realized that her own MgRonald—her castle, as she liked to think of it—was just ahead. All the other shops lined up nearby seemed completely different to her now.

"Well, I must be off! And don't worry! I'm sure you will find another wonderful space to rent!"

"...Yeah."

His encouragement usually rankled her, but this time, Kisaki meekly accepted it. She unlocked the back-door employee entrance, gritting her teeth a bit to refocus.

However, her cell phone started ringing. Taking it out, she raised an eyebrow at the name on the screen. It was from a regional coordinator, a level up in MgRonald bureaucracy from area manager. It wasn't unheard of for him to call Kisaki, but it was rare.

"Hello, this is Kisaki. Ah, yes, good morning... Oh? This afternoon? Certainly, my shifts are pretty well covered, so I can ask, but... What?"

His topic of conversation was something Kisaki was utterly unprepared for.

"...Um, me?"

The results of Sadao Maou's managerial training would be released a week later.

The agent had called not long after to inform her that the space was now taken. "Well," she had said to him over the phone, not particularly crestfallen, "sorry we couldn't do business this time. Let me know if you have any other good spaces." But she was still stopping by every now and then—this time, curious about what kind of shop had taken up residence there.

"Marko's friend said it'd make a good beauty salon..."

Kisaki couldn't see into the space, but judging by the paper covering the windows, the new tenant must have been doing some extensive renovations before opening up.

"Based on the signage," she muttered to herself, "it could be a chain, but I don't want to go prodding around too much..."

"Ah! I'd recognize that back anywhere! It's Ms. Kisaki!!"

"Bpph!"

The almost coquettish shout behind her made Kisaki choke on her coffee. She turned around, and as she expected, there was Mitsuki Sarue, not an ounce of regret evident in his sparkling eyes. It hadn't occurred to her until now, but she knew he lived somewhere nearby.

"...You're the last person I wanted to see this early in the morning."

"With *this* encounter, I'm now ready to tackle all the day's adversity with a smile!"

"Yeah, yeah."

Having this man prattle on about himself like always filled Kisaki with ennui. But she didn't want this chance to go to waste.

"Sarue, lemme ask you a question."

"Yes! Anything!"

"You live close to here, right? What kind of store is opening up in there?"

"There? Oh, that space?"

Thanks to a previous encounter or two, Sarue was aware that Kisaki was considering running her own place—and that she was scoping out potential retail spaces now and again.

"I believe it's a pizzeria. They put a flier in my mailbox not long ago."

"...A pizzeria?"

"Yes. A Dombino Pizza, I think. That's the chain that gives you a free pizza if you pick it up, right?"

The answer Sarue gave struck Kisaki like a thunderbolt. Her eyes turned downward. She crushed the empty coffee cup in her hand.

"Ugghhh... Why didn't *that* ever occur to me?"

"Er, how do you mean?"

"Never mind," she said—but inside, she was disturbed. Maou's friend Ashiya knew the space and its surroundings well. Many of the residents in the nearby apartments and condos were single people who wouldn't regularly visit a sit-down restaurant, and the roads around it didn't lend themselves to easy customer access. It wasn't much of a "destination" neighborhood, as he put it, and Kisaki readily agreed.

THE DEVIL IS A PART-TIMER!

SATOSHI WAGAHARA

ILLUSTRATED BY  029 (ONIKU)

17

YEN ON

NEW YORK

THE DEVIL IS A PART-TIMER!, Volume 17
SATOSHI WAGAHARA, ILLUSTRATION BY 029 (ONIKU)

Translation by Kevin Gifford
Cover art by 029 (oniku)

This book is a work of fiction. Names, characters, places, and incidents are the product of the author's imagination or are used fictitiously. Any resemblance to actual events, locales, or persons, living or dead, is coincidental.

HATARAKU MAOUSAMA!, Volume 17
© Satoshi Wagahara 2017
Edited by Dengeki Bunko
First published in Japan in 2017 by KADOKAWA CORPORATION, Tokyo.
English translation rights arranged with KADOKAWA CORPORATION,
Tokyo, through TUTTLE-MORI AGENCY, INC., Tokyo.

English translation © 2020 by Yen Press, LLC

Yen On
150 West 30th Street, 19th Floor
New York, NY 10001

Visit us at yenpress.com
facebook.com/yenpress
twitter.com/yenpress
yenpress.tumblr.com
instagram.com/yenpress

First Yen On Edition: September 2020

Yen On is an imprint of Yen Press, LLC.
The Yen On name and logo are trademarks of Yen Press, LLC.

The publisher is not responsible for websites (or their content) that are not owned by the publisher.

Library of Congress Cataloging-in-Publication Data
Names: Wagahara, Satoshi. | 029 (Light novel illustrator)
illustrator. | Gifford, Kevin, translator. | Steinbach, Kevin,
translator.
Title: The devil is a part-timer! / Satoshi Wagahara ;
illustration by 029 (oniku) : translation by Kevin Gifford,
translation by Kevin Steinbach. English
Other titles: Hataraku Maousama!. English
Description: First Yen On edition. | New York, NY :
Yen On, 2015-
Identifiers: LCCN 2015028390 |
ISBN 9780316383127 (v. 1 : pbk.) |
ISBN 9780316385015 (v. 2 : pbk.) |
ISBN 9780316385022 (v. 3 : pbk.) |
ISBN 9780316385039 (v. 4 : pbk.) |
ISBN 9780316385046 (v. 5 : pbk.) |
ISBN 9780316385060 (v. 6 : pbk.) |
ISBN 9780316469364 (v. 7 : pbk.) |
ISBN 9780316473910 (v. 8 : pbk.) |
ISBN 9780316474184 (v. 9 : pbk.) |
ISBN 9780316474207 (v. 10 : pbk.) |
ISBN 9780316474238 (v. 11 : pbk.) |
ISBN 9780316474252 (v. 12 : pbk.) |
ISBN 9780316474252 (v. 13 : pbk.) |
ISBN 9780316474252 (v. 14 : pbk.) |
ISBN 9781975302658 (v. 14 : pbk.) |
ISBN 9781975302672 (v. 15 : pbk.) |
ISBN 9781975302696 (v. 16 : pbk.) |
ISBN 9781975302719 (v. 16 : pbk.) |
ISBN 9781975302733 (v. 17 : pbk.)
Subjects: CYAC: Fantasy.
Classification: LCC PZ7.1.W34 Ha 2015 | DDC
[Fic]—dc23
LC record available at http://lccn.loc.
gov/2015028390

ISBNs: 978-1-9753-0273-3 (paperback)
978-1-9753-0274-0 (ebook)

1 3 5 7 9 10 8 6 4 2

LSC-C

Printed in the United States of America

OPENING

There exists a guardian spirit by the name of Asura. A benevolent god from ancient India, he was, through the winding path of history, adopted by Buddhism. In Japan, he was best known in his three-faced, six-armed *sanmen-roppi* form, as seen in a statue at the Kofuku-ji temple in Nara, which Japan's government certified as a National Treasure. By extension, *sanmen-roppi* had become an expression in the Japanese language meaning "someone who does the work of many."

And right now, at a MgRonald in the Sasazuka neighborhood of Tokyo's Shibuya ward, a man was acting as the true embodiment of that term.

"W-wow... The fries are *glowing*..."

They were. Fresh out of the deep fryer, they sparkled like gold ingots, thanks to his handiwork.

"We didn't replace the griddle tops, did we...?"

He had cleaned the clamshell grills that cooked the burgers, polishing them to a like-new shine.

"This one customer walked in so exhausted, but he was practically skipping out the door when he was done... We didn't put any 'special sauce' on our food today or anything, right?"

All the customers who'd eaten a certain someone's value meals left energized, ready to face the day.

When the staff began tracing the cause of each phenomenon, all fingers pointed toward Sadao Maou, an A-level MgRonald crewmember if ever there was one.

"Freaky."

Everyone who had ever worked a shift at the MgRonald near Hatagaya Station knew that Sadao Maou was dedicated to his job. Today, however, his work ethic was simply off the charts. One moment, you'd see him manning the front counter; the next, he was cooking burgers on the griddle; and by the time they were done, he had the drinks for five different value sets ready. Then, *whoosh*, he's got his helmet on as he sprints out for an order delivery—and then he's upstairs, whipping out his crowd-pleasing coffee in the café space.

"Is—is my eyesight failing me?" asked veteran crewmember Akiko Ohki, rubbing her eyes. "Because it looks like there are three or four Maous in the kitchen today."

"Marko's using bike number three for deliveries today," a visibly pale Takefumi Kawata added, "but his gas tank's still full. He couldn't have had the free time to fill up…"

"Yusa, could this be…?"

And of course, nobody was more concerned about Maou in the kitchen than Chiho Sasaki. Maou, in her eyes, was clearly acting strange. These things went beyond extraordinary and into the realm of supernatural, and they were all happening at once. It made her worry that Maou was tapping into his "real" powers to improve his performance.

She turned to Emi Yusa—her trusted friend and mentor (even though Chiho had worked there longer), and the only other person at the MgRonald to know Maou's "secret"—but Emi pensively shook her head.

"I don't sense any demonic force at all, no," she whispered back.

"It's not the *other* thing, is it?"

"What do you mean, 'the other thing'?"

Like a prophet from a biblical tract, Maou was performing miracles. Everywhere he went, there was clean equipment, purified griddles, and customers energized by greasy fast food as if they were eating something trendy from an upscale supermarket. If Maou wasn't harnessing his demonic force, the only thing Chiho could surmise was that Emi was using her holy magic to engineer this performance for some reason.

"Look, either way, demonic force is harmful to people. This is all just his 'human' self at work."

"The human body's got so much latent potential..."

"That's not exactly how I'd describe this."

Emi didn't think it was appropriate to liken Maou's potential, as a demon from another world, to a human's. And as Asura-like as his job performance today was, this wasn't any noble tale of someone gaining superhuman strength in the face of severe adversity.

Then their boss passed by with a confused expression.

"Oh, hello, Ms. Kisaki."

Mayumi Kisaki, manager of the Hatagaya Station MgRonald, turned her attractive face toward her possessed employee. She frowned.

"He's still at it, huh?"

"Still?"

"It'd be a miracle to stay that active for even half a day. Look."

Her eyes motioned toward the batch of fries Maou had just finished up. Chiho and Emi followed her gaze.

""Ah...""

The basket was glowing a golden yellow a moment ago—but now they were the same old MgRonald fries as always. And the griddles weren't forged from platinum or anything—they were the well-worn grayish color of stainless steel, like always. The customers were back to normal, distractedly shuffling off after finishing their meals.

"Wait... What?"

Then they noticed Maou himself. He looked, to be frank, dulled. Not sick or anything, but dulled. The three-faced Asura was back to the single-faced Sadao Maou—the same as he always was, but compared to his Asura fugue state, it seemed so lackluster.

And by the time Chiho and Emi's shift wrapped up at ten that evening:

"Whoa! Maou? Are you okay?!"

"You overdid it this afternoon, didn't you?" Emi scolded, rolling her eyes as Chiho panicked. Their alarm was understandable; Maou barely had a presence in the room. It even seemed like his bright-red MgRonald uniform had faded to a duller color.

"Oh, hey, Chi. Good job today. I'm fine. Got two more hours."

Chiho's voice restored a little color to his face, but he was still in the danger zone. If he lost his focus, he would deflate like a leaking balloon.

"Careful on the way home, okay?" he said. "Keep a close eye on her, Emi."

"S-sure..." Chiho offered.

"She's a lot more capable of defending herself right now than *you* are," Emi spat back.

Maou staggered back to work, not reacting to (perhaps not even hearing) Emi's sass.

"What happened to Maou...?"

"If I had to guess..."

Emi already had an idea to answer to Chiho's nervous question. But before she stated it, Kisaki put her hands on both of their shoulders.

"I'll watch him, okay? It's a manager's job to *care* for her staff's work-related stress."

She put extra emphasis on the word *care* as her eyes met Emi's.

"...All right. Thanks."

"Um, thanks," Chiho said, raising an eyebrow as Emi turned away.

"Sure. Take care on the way home."

Kisaki followed Maou upstairs. Emi and Chiho watched her go for a moment.

"Well, shall we?"

They went out into Sasazuka, the winter air finally beginning to break a bit. The night wind blew against their fatigued faces, making Chiho shiver and Emi sigh.

"Do you think Maou is worried about Camio?" Chiho asked, looking back toward the MgRonald as she walked. "I sure hope he goes back to normal soon."

"Yeah," Emi replied. There wasn't much feeling to her voice. Chiho had little to worry about, probably, but in Emi's mind, the situation was serious for completely different reasons. Serious for Maou, likely serious for Emi, but *definitely* serious for anyone in Ente Isla at the moment.

"Man oh man..."

Up until now, things had been going fairly well for Emi, in a way. This time, though, one false move and she might have a situation there'd be no taking back.

"If *this* winds up dictating the trend for our world, that's gonna drive me crazy."

"Marko?"

Most people are gifted with an instinct that tells them what topic people are about to discuss, based on the timing and tone of their voice. For what was likely the first time since he came to Japan, Maou could sense that *this* topic was one he wanted to run away from as quickly as possible. He tried his best to form a reply, feeling like a prisoner in front of the gallows.

"Uh."

"I wanted to talk to you about something. Do you have a little time after work?"

The words sent out from Kisaki's well-formed lips were nothing like what he expected.

".........What?"

"Just an hour-ish is fine. At this time of night... Why don't we hit that *izakaya* nearby again? I promise we won't run into any nosy friends of mine this time."

"Umm..."

Maou was still less than interested, but at least Kisaki had kept it under her hat. She had waited until after Chiho and Emi had left to bring this up; apparently she didn't want Kawata and Akiko downstairs listening in, either. Still, Kisaki wasn't done yet.

"It's really just this personal thing, you know. Nothing to get worked up about. I just want you to let me buy you dinner and listen to me whine for a while... I'm not making this sound appealing, am I?"

"Oh, no, um..." It was like she was reading Maou's mind. "I'm not in early tomorrow, so... Plus, I would have needed to make something for dinner tonight, so I'd actually appreciate that."

He meant it, too.

"Great. After we close, okay?" With a satisfied nod, she quietly retired to the staff room.

"It's about *that*, isn't it?" he whispered to himself.

She had called it whining, but that was likely just an excuse to get him to play along. It was very likely about *that*, actually. But would Kisaki play roundabout games with him concerning it?

"...Well, if it saves me from having to cook tonight, I'll play along."

No point stewing over it. He had to keep himself together right now, or else he'd be totally incapable of putting in his regular work effort.

"...*Man*, today's rough."

"Hey, Chiho, did you get all nervous when you were taking your high school entrance exams?"

"Where'd *that* come from?"

"Oh, I just mean... You know how the Devil King was acting weird today, right?"

"Right."

"I just thought he'd be on edge since he's gonna hear if he got picked up for the managerial track pretty soon. I've never really been in a situation where I had to wait on a job evaluation, so I was just wondering what it's like."

"Ah... Yeah, it did make me pretty nervous. Based on my practice exams, I knew I had a good shot at getting into Sasahata North. But it wasn't a slam dunk, either, so I took an exam for another private place, too, as my safety school."

"Your what now?"

Chiho gave Emi a surprised look, before realizing she probably didn't know the expression. "Oh, um, like a backup choice. A lot of people take entrance exams for two or three schools, just in case they don't get into their first choice."

Emi felt a little embarrassed that she didn't know the term. It seemed common enough, looking back, although she had never heard of it.

"Oh. A safe school... It'd be nice to always have a backup like that, huh?"

"Yusa?"

Emi seemed a little down to Chiho. Realizing this, Emi tried to sound more cheerful.

"I mean, like, here I am in this struggle to defeat the kinda-sorta god of an entire planet, but for now I've got a lot of time on my hands, you know? So I was starting to think I could start studying a little bit, too, but now the Devil King's acting funny. And it made me think exams must be really tough, huh?"

She knew her act wasn't very convincing, but Chiho seemed to buy it. Her eyes started to sparkle.

"Wait, you mean you're gonna go to school in Japan?!"

Chiho recalled when Emi, a little torn about her future, visited the home of her ex-coworker Maki Shimizu to talk about Japanese universities.

"Oh, it's nothing set in stone yet. But once I'm done with all this, I'll need to start thinking about afterward, you know?"

Emi's pace of speech was a little faster than usual. She didn't know if Chiho noticed. But then Chiho took Emi's arm and brought it to her face, in a sort of caress.

"Hey, what're you doing?"

"Hee-hee! Oh, I'm just happy for you, Yusa. It's like you're starting to move in the right direction."

"Oh? What's *that* mean? Let me remind you, I haven't totally divorced myself from my mission to slay the Devil King yet."

"Right, right, I knooooow. I *think* I heard you say you weren't gonna fight anymore, but..."

Emi knew she wasn't convincing Chiho at all. But she said it anyway. Otherwise, it'd feel like Chiho had her wrapped around her little finger, and that peeved her. Nonetheless, Emi didn't pull her arm away, staying close to her as they walked down the Koshu-Kaido sidewalk.

"But I also think…"

That must have been why Chiho's voice was so clear and crisp in her ears, looming over the sounds of background traffic.

"…you might be drifting kind of far away."

Chiho was perceptive. Behind that simple sentence were layers of consideration. Emi couldn't be sure of it, but she had the impression Chiho knew exactly why Kisaki had acted the way she had today, as well as why Emi had asked the question she just did.

She *thought* she knew…and that was why she pretended not to.

"Did he do something mean to you again, Chiho?"

"Nothing more than usual. I'm used to it."

Chiho half meant it. Emi laughed in response, making Chiho give her a resentful smile—and so, implicitly, they moved away from the essence of their issues.

It had all begun yesterday, when a single envelope in the mailbox for Room 201 of Villa Rosa Sasazuka—the postwar-era wooden apartment building in a corner of Shibuya ward—was on the verge of making all the building's inhabitants wail in unison.

The envelope was from the Human Resources Department at the Tokyo headquarters of the MgRonald Corporation in Japan. It was addressed to Sadao Maou, and it felt thick and solid to the touch, but inside was nothing but a standard sheet of paper.

Dear Sadao Maou,

Thank you for applying for the managerial assignment program at MgRonald. After careful deliberation, we regret to announce that we are not accepting your application at this time.

Our program accepts only a small number of people from a wealth of applications, and we regret that we could not add you to the program. Nonetheless, we thank you for your application, and we hope that you will continue your outstanding service as a crewmember for a long time to come.

Sincerely,
Satoru Kojima
Employment Agent

THE DEVIL KING GOES OUT TO DINNER WITH HIS BOSS

The air in Room 201 of Villa Rosa Sasazuka was still penetratingly cold when Maou stepped inside, careful not to make any noise. Turning on the fluorescent light in the kitchen, he looked around his one-room apartment, which was a bit dim and yellowed thanks to the old light cover. They hadn't really acquired a lot of things since they first came to Japan, but now, in the corner farthest away from the light, there was a large box on the floor.

Maou peeked inside, then let out a small, relieved sigh.

"…You're alive, huh?"

Inside was a very large and plump-looking chicken…or to be more exact, Camio, the arch-demon and de facto father figure to Maou.

"Peep…chrr…peep…chrr…"

He listened to Camio sleep a bit, taking shallow but rhythmic breaths, as he sat in front of the box. Then, recalling the crumpled-up MgRonald notice he tossed in the nearby wastebasket, he sighed.

"Ugh… How did I mess it up with them?"

He wasn't being conceited. He honestly didn't suspect for a single moment that he'd be turned down. It was smooth sailing through every screening. His rivals were shot down, one by one, and he made it all the way to the final selection process. For applicants from the shift-employee ranks at MgRonald (as opposed to new hires from college), this meant an interview with a company executive—and he was confident about his interview skills, as well as the assorted roles he played in the group discussions. He had tirelessly researched the industry as well.

Only about a quarter of the applicants made it as far as the executive interview. Maou was among them, and by that point, he was sure he hadn't made a single misstep. But they turned him down. They didn't reveal their screening standards, of course, and they didn't explain why they gave him a pass.

"Where did I go wrong…?"

Maou kept his moaning to a quiet murmur, so as not to wake up Camio. Griping wouldn't accomplish anything. It wouldn't change reality. But the experience of being rejected with a single thin sheet of paper hurt nonetheless.

"It's been like this with everything lately."

Things were not going the way he wanted.

That didn't bother him if everything worked out successfully in the end, as it did with the Spear of Adramelechinus. But failing to earn a career-track job at MgRonald was a failure like none before.

"…I'll need a bath before tomorrow's shift."

Having a dream he'd held close to his heart ever since his first shift at MgRonald crushed like this weighed heavily on the Devil King of another world. He lifted that heavy heart upward, coming to his feet. It was time to prepare for bed…but as he got up, he noticed that his futon was still laid out on the floor, instead of folded up and in the closet.

"Oh. I didn't put it away this morning?"

He tried to remember, but the shock of receiving that rejection notice in the morning blurred his memory. Based on how unfolded and messy the comforter was, he must've left it that way.

"Ashiya would ream me for being so messy if he were here. I should get some sleep for now… Hmm?"

Then he noticed. There were no pillows.

"Hmmmm? Where are they? And my pajamas… Huh?"

If he'd woken up and left the room unattended this morning, both of those things should have been right in front of him. But they weren't.

"Did I only put those away? Would I even do that?"

Maou frowned as he opened one of the closet doors.

"Oh, hey, you're back."

"Aaaah?!"

Hanzou Urushihara, Master of the Closet, was lying down in front of him. "Dude, what?" he spat, lowering his headphones as he eyed Maou, who had fallen on the floor in shock. "I'm not *that* surprising."

"Yes, you are! If you're home, say something! I thought you were a burglar!"

"Why would the Devil King be afraid of a burglar? And for the record, I didn't notice you were home at all, either, and you don't see me screaming."

"Yeah, I kept quiet because I don't want to wake up Camio! Besides, you didn't hear anything because you had those headphones on... Wait, where'd you get those headphones?"

At the moment, Urushihara's unannounced return to his closet when he shouldn't be in Japan at all wasn't as important as the wireless headphones he had on. His laptop was bathing the closet space in a pale-blue light.

"Oh, these? I got here this afternoon, so I ordered them same-day delivery from Jungle. They're pretty good."

"Wow, impulse shopping online? Just like the good old days! What the hell are you back here for anyway? Without even warning me!"

"What's the big deal, dude? Things are pretty chill over there, now that we got the Spear. We rounded up most of the surviving demons on the Central Continent, and the Malebranche are keepin' them all disciplined and stuff, so I thought I'd take a break and screw around over here for a bit."

"I can't believe you... Wait, what happened to the demonic force I stored in the closet?"

"Oh, yeah, it was takin' up too much space, so I moved it out to

the far end of the hallway. That's why all the futon crap is out on the floor, by the way."

"Do you have *any* goddamn common sense whatsoever?!"

Not only had he palmed off all of his Ente Isla responsibility on other people, but Urushihara had also committed the cardinal sin of using Maou's credit card. But the rage bubbling within Maou was almost a welcome feeling for him. Nostalgia, perhaps, reminding him of who he truly was.

"...*Chweep...ngh...*"

And with all the shouting, nobody noticed that Camio had repositioned himself in his box a little. Still, he remained asleep.

✳

Their united mission was to storm the blue moon orbiting Ente Isla and attack the angels that controlled the planet's history from behind the scenes. Maou and company had signed up for this god-slaying struggle, which involved restoring Devil's Castle on Ente Isla and launching it like a spaceship toward heaven. To do that, they needed four sacred relics—the Nothung, the Sorcery of the False Gold, the Spear of Adramelechinus, and the Astral Gem.

The Spear was their most recent find, discovered on Ente Isla's Northern Island, where it served as a monument commemorating victory over the Devil King's Army. Satan, the Devil King, and Emilia the Hero were leading this struggle, accompanied by a large group of allied humans and demons, but this alliance wasn't the sort of thing that could be publicized to the world. If they seized the Spear by force, then whether they succeeded or not, they ran the risk of sowing the seeds for future wars.

Maou and Emi were the flag bearers for this effort, but there was nothing among the preparations they could contribute to, so they kept up with their jobs in Sasazuka. On the other hand, Suzuno Kamazuki, Laila, Albert, and Saint Aile's General Rumack were all involved in the negotiations with Dhin Dhem Wurs, chief herder of the Northern Island and bearer of a Yesod fragment. A longtime acquaintance of Laila's, Wurs understood the importance of this heavenly struggle and promised her cooperation in supplying the Spear to them. This was done in the midst of a zirga, a part-ceremony, part–sporting event to decide the next chief herder, and Chiho Sasaki posed as Wurs's granddaughter to participate.

The (literally) trans-dimensional archery skills she showed off at the event's climax, the Bowman's Offering, astounded the crowd. Her arrow, supported by the lingering magic from the long-gone Adramelech, had summoned a spear of ice up from the ground. As it did, Suzuno and Laila had transported the real Spear of Adramelechinus away, while Malebranche chieftain Libicocco had used his illusionary skills to summon a living image of its namesake. The way average Northern Islanders heard it in the rumors, Adramelech had come back from the dead to fetch the spear he left behind.

Maou played no part of any of this, which irked him, but as far as he was concerned, all's well that ends well. That just left the Astral Gem to track down.

Chiho, back in Japan after her now-legendary actions in Ente Isla, later discovered a seriously wounded Camio in her front yard, bereft of his magic force and back in chicken mode. The guardian angel Camael was hot on his heels, wielding his three-pronged spear and ready to tear down the Sasaki family house with it, but the day was saved by Amane Ohguro, part of the Sephirot on Earth. Everyone was safe, but the ordeal put a pall on the whole relic search that still hadn't cleared out.

It certainly made for an exciting start to March, as winter slowly slipped away from the Tokyo landscape.

✳

"So what, dude? I know you look pretty down and all, but did that one-page rejection letter really depress you *that* much?"

Maou was seated on the floor, listening to Urushihara's quiet lecturing from the closet.

"I almost wish that was the case, but that's not the only thing I got going on tonight..."

"What, there's more? Something else that could make the Devil King mope like a baby?"

"Shut up. It's been like a one-two punch for me, okay?"

"Huhhh?"

Urushihara naturally knew about the career aspirations Maou had since he came to Japan. He could understand that kind of rejection taking the wind out of his sails. But he couldn't think of anything else that could bring him down so hard.

"Look, don't tell anyone yet, okay? Not that you have anyone you *could* tell, except Emi and Chi, but..."

Maou heaved a sigh. "Kisaki's getting transferred."

"Ohhh."

"...'Ohhh'? That's all you've got to say??"

In a way, the news that Hatagaya Station MgRonald manager Mayumi Kisaki had received a transfer order sucker-punched Maou even more than his rejection had. It was akin to removing the very backbone of that MgRonald location. That was why Urushihara's reaction—going beyond indifference and well into the realm of spite—sincerely annoyed Maou.

"That sort of thing happens all the time, dude," he offered nonchalantly. "Staff get moved around in chain restaurants a ton, don't they? Plus, I dunno Kisaki, but she's supposed to be really talented, right? If she's worked there long enough, maybe at this point she's gonna get automatically promoted."

Maou watched, mouth agape, as the still-disinterested Urushihara snorted at him.

"Why're you looking at me like that, man?"

"Uh, no," replied Maou, "I'm just surprised at how right you are, even though you almost never do any work."

"I'll be expecting an apology, dude, once you see how hard I'm workin' in Ente Isla. I think a ten-thousand-yen Jungle gift card'll help me forgive you."

The fallen angel's consumer-minded bribery aside, Kisaki's

situation *was* a common one. She'd said so herself; if anything, it was odd that she hadn't been moved from the Hatagaya Station outlet until now. Their MgRonald was once on the smaller side, compared to the average location, and its revenues were commensurate with that when Kisaki joined. But with her at the helm, sales had continually risen year after year—and they had even expanded into the second floor of the building they rented. That was why their location was almost always picked for pilot projects like the café and the delivery system—because Kisaki and the crew she trained always gave the company solid results.

✳

"I must've done too well. The higher-ups had their eye on me…in a good *and* a bad way."

Kisaki swirled the ice in her glass of oolong tea around and snickered.

"Had their eye on you…?"

Kisaki would transfer out at the end of the fiscal year—by April 1. Maou was too shocked to offer much besides that instinctual reaction.

"In a good way, because it meant a big promotion to me. Do you remember my old friend who tried to start stuff with me at our location?"

If it was a "big promotion," Kisaki didn't seem so happy about it.

"Yeah, Tanaka from Sentucky. How could I forget?"

Himeko Tanaka was both an area manager for Sentucky Fried Chicken and Kisaki's childhood friend. That made her the boss of Mitsuki Sarue, aka Sariel the archangel—a business rival of Maou's in two separate ways.

"In terms of job ranking, this is gonna leapfrog me right past her. Not that it means much more of a paycheck in *this* industry, but it's gonna change the job title on my business card to something fancy-sounding."

Himeko and Kisaki were dyed-in-the-wool rivals for all time.

They had known each other since they were children, but neither would dare use the term *friend* to refer to their current relationship. If they were in the same room, the slightest provocation could result in a knock-down-drag-out between the two of them. But again, if Kisaki was now ahead of her on the career track, she didn't look at all excited about it.

"So what about in a bad way?"

"I'll stop being involved with day-to-day restaurant operations. I'm not going to some other location or area. I'm joining the Consumer Insight Team."

"The Consumer Insight Team?!"

The term was invented for the advertising industry toward the end of the twentieth century. Now, it was an indispensable concept when building diverse relationships with businesses and consumers, in every aspect of corporate management.

While marketing and planning work would sometimes get mixed in with consumer insight at a company, the essence of the term actually referred to something earlier on in the business process: Basically, in the real world, sometimes a good product doesn't sell well, while the most popular products aren't always the best ones. You might find true gems among unpopular products, or you might find that products that were no good to start out with later had improved in quality.

There were exceptions, of course, but in the long run, it was a given in any industry that if a product was vastly superior to the competition, it'd likely gain massive support in the market. But that didn't mean all the companies in the world should just develop one excellent product and sell that for all time. In a capitalist society, a company was obligated to pursue profits—but outside of that iron-clad rule, the fundamentals of business management were rapidly changing.

Toward that end, the job of a consumer insight department was to research the hooks that connected a company to a customer in an age when mass marketing was gradually waning as a force in advertising, then feed those hooks back into every aspect of the company and indirectly contribute to its bottom line. Such hooks could be more than just things like product quality and price; for example, a company being mired in scandal could affect consumers' purchasing decisions. If the firm took it seriously and held a press conference to apologize, consumers might become anxious and stop buying the product, which hurt profits. On the other hand, if PR execs running official social media accounts picked humorous fights with rival companies online, it could spread like wildfire and often improve the company's brand image. A good consumer insight team analyzed these trends and fed their findings into the company's operations across the board.

Their actual work wasn't that simple, of course, but basically, Kisaki's new department continually researched which products, ads, behaviors, aspects, attitudes, or strategies either attracted consumer eyeballs or made them turn away.

As someone who underwent managerial training, Maou naturally had the MgRonald organizational chart memorized. Thanks to that knowledge, he knew that a promotion from a store manager to the Consumer Insight Team was all but unimaginable. That was why he was so shocked.

"We've done a lot at our location, you know?"

"Yeah. The café and deliveries, one after the other."

"So I guess they liked what they saw. Plus, I bet they want to get some on-the-field data from me. The sites I've run are near the top of the company in both sales and crew retention. Hatagaya Station, in particular, is just off the charts. Our new features were hitting their sales goals in half the time we were projected to."

Maou knew that. It came up in their business meetings.

"The Consumer Insight Team is still kind of in the experimental phase. It's pretty new, and most of the staff are on the younger side. It's led by a woman in her forties, and they're trying to get as many people as they can. Normally, I'd be promoted to an area manager, but that team plucked me up instead... Hey, eat up, okay? I'm gonna be pretty much bragging for the next little while. It's gonna get uncomfortable fast if you don't eat on my dime."

"Oh, sorry. Thanks. Um, oolong tea... No, I mean jasmine tea."

Maou was so caught up in the conversation that he barely even noticed the assorted fried appetizers on the table. Realizing his nerves were making him thirsty, he ordered a refill on his tea.

"I guess you don't drink, either, huh, Marko? I remember someone telling me that."

"Either?"

"Aki and Kawacchi don't drink, usually. Not that they can't, but they choose not to."

"Well, maybe there's just nothing they want to drink that bad when they're going out. Like, the stuff they like is expensive or whatever."

"That was kind of how Kawacchi put it, yeah. Of course, he's got that motorcycle, so I'm sure that's where he puts a lot of his money."

"But you don't drink that much, either, do you, Ms. Kisaki?"

"Mm... Well, like Himeko said that one time, it makes my face all red almost immediately. Plus, if I drink tonight, I have a feeling I'm gonna spend all night bitching about my life."

She *did* describe this as a "whining" session earlier. For the time being, it still sounded like her bragging about a big promotion. She worked hard, delivered results, and got picked for a strategic-planning position from the front lines. And while she downplayed how much more her paycheck would be, there had to be *some* kind of raise. But she still seemed reluctant about it.

"So," Kisaki said suddenly as Maou thought that over, "what do you think of consumer insight?"

"I don't think it fits you."

This brutally honest appraisal made Kisaki do something she never, ever did on the clock—laugh uproariously.

"Ha-ha-ha-ha-ha! Right? You're totally right! This doesn't fit me at all. I mean, it's not like the team is 'Ohh, consumer insight, consumer insight' all day. They do *some* on-the-ground stuff, too. But like..."

"You don't like not seeing your customers' faces."

"Right! Exactly!"

She might not have been drinking, but Kisaki was still acting pretty intense.

Maou never asked her directly, but Kisaki was twenty-seven or twenty-eight this year. In Japan's business culture, that was still considered young. And given how aloof and detached she acted at his workplace, Maou felt like he was getting a taste of Kisaki actually acting her age.

"When I first heard about this, I didn't think I was suited for it. Like, HR must think I am or else none of this would be happening, so I'm not gonna say 'No way,' but…"

Thinking you're unsuited for something was much different from actually *being* unsuited for it. Kisaki understood that. That must have been why she had that ambiguous expression.

"And I knew this was coming, but now that I'm actually going to be in that position, of course that's gonna make me start to think about it again."

"Think about what?"

"You know. I told you about my dream, didn't I?"

She hadn't been secretive about it. She had told Maou, Chiba, Emi, and even Sarue about her dream of running her own place—a café and bar, in the Italian tradition.

"I like being on the floor…but as much as I wanted to deny it, that's just not enough. I think this is a necessary step on the way to that dream."

"A necessary step?"

He never thought he'd see that emotion from Kisaki. But it was clear as day on her face—her anxiety for the future.

"*Ugghh!* Why can't we just have a world where you make nice things, and people buy lots of them, and that's *it*, Marko?"

"Huh? Um…"

"Marko! Which do you like more on your yakitori? Sauce or salt?"

"Uh? S-sauce, I guess, if it's one of the two."

"I like salt!"

"Oh? Don't you wind up tasting the salt a lot more than the chicken?"

"But that yakitori sauce is just a big sweetness bomb. Bad sauce can ruin chicken in a way bad salt never does."

In the end, Kisaki used her powers as Maou's boss to order… chicken wings, for some reason, in a sweet-and-salty sauce.

"See? It's something so simple, and we can't even agree on that! What does being 'good' even mean? What does 'selling' something even mean?!"

"…Well, I just hope these chicken wings turn out well. I've never had them prepared like this before."

"Right! Right there! Encouraging consumers to challenge themselves with new things! With Japan in a deflationary period, what's it take to sell stuff when people are so tight with their wallets? I think about it and think about it, and I come up with a solution and throw it out as all wrong three hours later. Can I *ever* go independent like this?"

They later engaged in a fiery debate over the chicken wings, but given the late hour, they didn't speak in-depth about much else before going their separate ways.

"See you later, okay? I know I don't have much time left here, but keep up the good work."

Right up to the end, Kisaki didn't even come close to mentioning Maou's application results. But the way she chose to say good-bye still felt like an arrow through the heart.

✳

"Oh, man, don't talk to me about yakitori and chicken wings in the middle of the night. You're making me hungry."

"*That's* the part you care about?"

"What else *could* I care about? It's not like I'm emotionally attached to Kisaki or anything, my dude."

This attachment, or lack thereof, was the classic reason why workplace complaints tended to fall on deaf ears at home.

"What?" Urushihara protested. "What do you want me to say, man?"

"At least prove to me you're worth the headphones you got on. I dunno how much they cost, but if you can actually give me a little help, I can let it slide."

"Oh? Wow. That's a good deal. Ashiya would've whined about these to me for the next ten days."

Maou's face was turned away, but he could tell Urushihara was smiling.

"But you know, things never change. You should know most of all, Maou, that things don't go the way they should in an ideal world. They sure haven't for *me*."

"Yeah, because you just mooch off everyone else."

"Hey, being an unemployed bum doesn't mean you're happy about your life. If I had a situation where I could use my abilities, I'd quit this life in a flash. But that sort of thing just doesn't come walkin' along, and I don't really feel like trying to *make* it come along. I don't think I *like* it or anything, but that's how I'm living."

"You can at least *try* to act apologetic about it. If you don't like it, act that way. You're not convincing me at all."

"If I acted all mopey, it'd just bring the energy down more. Don't you see I'm doing this for you?"

"You really know how to drive me insane, you know that?"

"Sure. And actually, I was thinking I better say this to you sooner or later…"

Maou could sense Urushihara dangling his legs down from his perch in the closet.

"Maou, don't you think you oughta quit with this Japan stuff soon? Is right now the time to be talking about Kisaki, or your 'career' or whatever you call it here?"

His voice was dead serious.

"I'm not criticizing His Honor, the Devil King, for this little side diversion he fell into after all the torment he went through, all right? But that's all it really is. A diversion. A hobby. Do you really *need* a career-track job for your life to be complete, Maou?"

"…"

"And you know, living in Japan is fun. I wouldn't mind keeping this apartment if it was a second home. And Chiho Sasaki and Rika Suzuki are…you know, I don't mind talking with them. But c'mon, do you absolutely *need* any of it? It's not gonna hurt anyone if you make Japan just someplace you send a New Year's card to every year. So if you want me to advise you or whatever, I'd say it's about time you went back to Ente Isla and started packing up your life here a little."

"…"

"And that's even more true if the reason you wanna stay involved with Japan is Chiho Sasaki or your boss or whatever. Because there's at least a few other people you should probably focus more of your attention on right now, you know? Oh, but…"

Urushihara clapped his hands.

"You know, if you *really* don't give a damn about Ente Isla any longer… Like, if you decided this is your main thing from now on, then fine. But you do give a damn, right?"

"…You really know how to twist the knife, don't you?"

"You told me to." Urushihara hopped out of the closet and crouched in front of the box Camio slept in. "'Cause beyond that, the only real obstacle is Emilia, isn't it?"

"Don't call her an obstacle. She'll kill you."

"Well, she is; let's not lie to ourselves. We're demons from the demon realms. Meanwhile, she's still got Emeralda, and Rumack, and Albert, and Bell. In the end, do you think you're gonna come to any kind of real understanding with them? You won't. And in the not too distant future—like, within a year—this holding pattern you're in is gonna come to a shuddering halt. That's what you and Emilia decided on, isn't it? That's what killing Ignora's gonna accomplish."

Once they lost their common goal, and their common enemy, their split would come soon after. They never got along very well to start with. If their paths started to diverge, it wouldn't take that much time for them to be at each other's throats once more.

"And while I'm at it, lemme just say, 'staying together for the kids' only works for so long. The fact that I'm still alive is proof enough of that."

Urushihara's parents—Ignora and Satanael—were supposed to be pursuing the same dreams. But for one reason or the other, they broke it off...and in the end, they fought each other. And they had Lucifer, their flesh and blood, but it wasn't enough to keep them together. Would Alas Ramus, "child" of Maou and Emi, function any better as a bond for them?

"Do you even remember when your parents split up?" Maou asked.

"No. Like I said, I barely remember anything. I'm not even sure I can tell you what they looked like. But in the end...I think it was Satanael who acted the most like a parent to me, really."

"Like a parent?"

"I...think he saved my life? Probably."

"You sound kinda unsure about it."

"I told you, my dude, I don't remember. Once Malacoda and his gang joined the Devil King's Army, I started remembering things from, like, when we boarded Satan's Ark for the first time. But it's all, like, sense memory. It's irritating. I don't really *remember* anything—or maybe I wanted to forget about it. But in the end, I know I was with Satanael. And who's it gonna be with Alas Ramus, huh?"

"I really don't want to have a custody battle. The father almost never wins those in Japan."

"Y'know, you really need to stop shoehorning the most important parts of your life into the framework of Japan and making a joke out of them."

"Stuff it."

"And how much time does old man Camio have left anyway? You should put his mind at ease already, you know."

"I *really* don't need you telling me that." Maou got to his feet and stepped closer to Camio's box. "If you were working *soooo* hard over in Ente Isla, then tell me this: Why did this happen to him? He was looking for the Astral Gem in the demon realms."

"I dunno. Chances are, he found it, but then Camael stuck his spear in where it didn't belong and whooped his ass. There *are* a few odd points about that, though."

"Yeah."

And as they watched the wizened old demon sleep in the card-board box, they both said in unison:

""Fight against Camael, and you'll never come back alive.""

Camael was a guardian angel from heaven. It was a given that he'd be at least as powerful as fellow guardian angel Gabriel. And before fusing with Acieth, Maou had no chance against Gabriel even in full demon mode. As old as he was, Camio was still incomparably more powerful than your average demon, but that still only made him a bit stronger than, say, a Malebranche chieftain. It was doubtful he and Camael knew each other. If such an overpowered angel came across Camio on the battlefield, he'd have no reason to spare the life of that old soldier. But why would he chase Camio all the way to Japan, get blocked by Amane Ohguro right when he was about to strike the final blow, then simply leave without further comment?

"The spear itself was Camael's, right?" Maou asked.

"Probably. We'd know for sure if Camio would just open his eyes already—not that I can blame him. What did Amane and Chiho Sasaki say to you?"

"Neither of them actually saw Camael."

"Hmm… What's up with that?"

"Either way, we're gonna have to be careful. I talked with Emi, and we agreed that she and Chi should share shifts as much as possible."

"…"

It was hard to believe Maou would say that after the conversation they had just moments ago. Urushihara gave him an exasperated sneer.

"What, you got a problem with that?"

"Hey, if you wanna use her, then use her while you still can, dude."

"Look, if you think I'm flying blind without thinking anything through, you're wrong."

"Sure, sure."

"Hey—"

"We found three out of four Devil Overlord's relics in no time flat. If heaven didn't make any moves at all during that time—why not,

I have no idea—but that's a seriously lucky break. So we better be prepared for a slog finding this fourth one. It'll make recovering the Spear look like a trip to the store."

"At least it'll be an easier slog for me to grasp this time…"

While they'd been searching for the Spear of Adramelechinus, they'd been obliged to keep careful tabs on the goings-on in the human world the whole time. Having Chiho's courage be the single unifying factor in the plan's success in the end—something Maou wasn't privy to until it was practically about to begin—mentally exhausted him.

"With this one, if someone's in our way, we kick their ass. Simple. And Acieth and I could whip a hundred Camaels all at once."

"It's not gonna be so easy. If you do fight him, where are you gonna do it? You don't want to have a huge epic battle in Japan, do you? But there's still a lot of people on the Central Continent who have no idea what's going on. Whether you got Acieth or not, if you fight using your Devil King–level force, people are gonna start flooding in."

"Maybe we could, like, set up a Gate to the south pole for it or something."

"That's a distressingly realistic-sounding idea, my dude. But I guess we're at the point where we'll need something like that, huh? And we're thinking about Camael right now, but there's still Raguel and a bunch of other annoying angels, too."

"Gabriel hinted that heaven didn't have that many useful pieces to work with. I wonder how true that is. He said there's about five thousand total, but it's not like they can all fight. Apart from you and the Heavenly Regiment guys, we've only really run into four of them—Sariel, Gabriel, Raguel, and Camael. That's kind of weird, if you think about it… Hmm?"

The phone in Maou's pocket vibrated.

"Pretty late to be receiving a text… Oh, Emi?"

"Sorry if you were sleeping," began her text—an oddly thoughtful thing for her to say to him. "I'm probably overthinking things, but when you get up, look at these—" followed by two web links.

"Hey, Urushihara, this isn't spam for a porn site or something, is it?"

"Huh?"

"Because it doesn't read like Emi's writing. At all."

"I'm shocked she even texts you. I know I shouldn't be at this point, but... Lemme see."

Urushihara raised an eyebrow at the URLs.

"The top one's a social media post—like, one of the photo-oriented ones. I think the bottom one's some kind of news site. Neither's gonna take you anywhere weird, I don't think. She's gonna bitch at you if you ignore her, so just open them."

"Social media... Yeah, they asked me for my online handles and stuff during the job-training interviews. I told them I wasn't on any, and they looked at me like I was insane."

"Oh. I figured that'd reflect on you better with the company, but they rejected you anyway, huh? So what're the links for?"

"Stop twisting the knife without warning me first, man. The first one is... Huh?"

Maou's eyebrows slanted downward as he checked his screen.

"An alligator?"

"What?"

"It's this post about how there's an alligator on the loose somewhere in Shibuya."

"Whaa? What're you talking about? ...Oh, whoa, you're right."

Urushihara, curious, had sidled next to him for a peek at the screen. But there was no other way to describe the photo. It was a night scene depicting some kind of large reptile from far away, with the caption Maou described.

"What's the other URL?"

"Same thing. Looks more like a forum than a news site, but there are a few posts from people saying they saw an alligator in Shibuya."

"Why would Emilia send you that?"

"How should I know? Can you use your computer to look this up? It's annoying to do on this little phone..."

"One sec. 'Shibuya,' 'alligator'... Yeah, it's just bringing up random posts for the most part. I think it's a fake, and people are trying to milk it for likes. I mean, dude, if this is a pic of an alligator, then it's *huge*."

Urushihara brought his laptop down from the closet. On the bigger screen, they could both see a mailbox-like object next to the crocodilian creature. Comparing their relative sizes, this gator was unlikely to fit in too many lakes in Japan.

"Is it fake? Isn't that bad, if you spread fake stuff like this on the net? If there was an alligator *this* big in Shibuya, it'd be huge news."

"A lot of people don't think it's bad at all. That's the problem. But it's weird…"

"Hmm?"

"Normally, if this was a onetime fake, maybe it'd get spread around a bunch, but that's the last you'd hear about this. But look."

Urushihara's voice gradually grew more serious.

"Here's a pic of the same alligator from a different angle…and a different poster."

"So multiple people saw this?"

"Someone might have arranged these posts just to make it seem more believable, but… Hmm. Why don't you try calling Emilia? Because if she thought it was alarming enough to tell you about—"

But before he could finish the sentence, Urushihara was cut short by the sensation of the Sasazuka air shuddering around them.

""?!""

"…*Peep*…"

Maou and Urushihara immediately looked up. It was far away, but they could feel it—the shock wave from an explosion. And not just any explosion.

"All right," Maou said with urgency. "Urushihara, you keep watch over Camio in here. I'm gonna call Emi and go check this out."

"Okay. I'll let Ashiya and Bell know, too."

"Thanks… Whoa?!"

"Huh?"

Then the front door, which they thought was locked, flew open, frightening both Maou and Urushihara.

"…Oh, Maou and the chicken are in here, huh?"

It was a slightly sleepy-eyed Amane Ohguro.

"And you're back, too, Urushihara? Where's Ashiya? Still over *there*, right? So what was that just now?"

"We don't know," Maou replied. "I was just about to go find out."

"So it wasn't you guys? Oh, this is the *last* thing I needed tonight! I was all snuggled up in bed and everything!"

Just as Maou exited the apartment, pushing the nagging Amane ahead of him, his phone rang. He didn't bother checking the screen.

"Hi. I'm just about to go to the scene with Amane. You?"

"I'm flying to Chiho's right now," Emi replied. "Good thing it's the middle of the night, at least."

"Thanks. Talk to you later."

"Yeah. You be careful, too."

Maou tossed the phone back in his pocket and jumped out of Room 201.

"Was that Yusa?" Amane groggily asked on the way down the stairs.

"Yeah, she said she's headed for Chi."

"Well, it's a good thing you're staying in contact."

"We need to. It helps."

"Wow, all business with you, huh? …No time for idle chatter right now, though."

She must have planned to poke more fun at Maou about that, but her face was already stiffening up when she said it.

"That's in the direction of Yoyogi Park, isn't it?"

Maou winced. The first alligator pic he saw seemed to have a lot of trees and grass, which was unusual for the cosmopolitan Shibuya ward. Everything was still far too unclear, but one thing was certain. The entire reason why Maou, Emi, and Amane were all outside—and why even Urushihara was willing to listen to his orders. The explosion had been a burst of demonic energy—but the only people on Earth who could even wield such power right now were Maou, Urushihara, and Camio.

"Can you fly?"

"I was about to ask you that."

With a leap, they were both in the air, headed for the site of the blast.

"This isn't your long-clawed demon lackey causing trouble again, is it?"

"If it is, I'm kicking him out of my force. Unfortunately, I'm imagining something a lot worse."

Maou looked at Amane's left hand. He heard she'd cut it pretty badly after stopping Camael's spear, but it had nothing but a small bandage on it.

"Listen, it's possible to use holy energy to create demonic energy inside the bodies of people on Earth."

The angel Raguel had once sent off a probing blast of holy energy to search for Laila after she'd come to Japan, hiding it within broadcast TV signals. Chiho had received a direct hit from it, and the reaction had created demonic energy within her body and knocked her unconscious for a whole day.

"Right, like when Chiho was in the hospital? That sounded kind of rough."

"There's a chance we'll run into an angel soon, and if there is, we better keep that in mind."

"Ugh, I wish we could just go up there and kill all of 'em at once!"

"I'll be happy to, if you want," Maou replied to the unusually bloodthirsty Amane. "It'd make things easier for us, too."

"Ah, don't be stupid. That'll just make it worse. Keep your Ente Isla problems in Ente Isla, please."

This late at night, neither was shy about flying—Maou harnessing his demonic energy, and Amane just…floating there, being held up by neither holy nor demonic force. It reminded Maou once again that she was definitely not a normal human.

"Is that it?"

"I think so."

There was a crater in a corner of Yoyogi Park, as if a small meteorite had hit the ground. The trees around it were on fire, and they were already starting to hear sirens in the distance. And the weirdest thing of all was the enormous creature in the middle of it. "Alligator" was the only real way to describe it, but it was far more gigantic than any alligator on Earth.

"Is that...a demon?"

It looked close enough to an alligator from far away, but between its horns, its fangs, and most of all its size, it was more like a previously undiscovered dinosaur species. Definitely not the kind of creature that could show up in the middle of Tokyo and *not* attract attention.

"Now what? The trains stopped running long ago, but it's attracting more and more cars and people..."

Already, a decent-sized crowd was on the scene, keeping a polite distance as they gawked at the creature.

"Don't they have anything better to do right now? ...Let me blindfold them real quick."

With a judgmental clicking of the tongue, he built a simple demonic barrier around him to cut off the crowd's visual.

"How 'bout we off this guy while we still can right now?"

"Cool it, please. I want to know why something like this is here."

"Well, it's not from Earth. And this crater is unnatural, too. If we leave it be, it's gonna kill someone."

Amane's eyes were as cold as ice. No, they had no idea what this thing was, and Maou had never seen a demon like it before. It was in the middle of the crater, looking around its surroundings and appearing incredibly lethal—and how was that crater made anyway?

"Sorry, but humans on Earth are always gonna take priority over creatures from another world with me."

Maou scowled. There was nothing he could say or do to stop Amane.

""?!""

The alligator stared straight at the two of them, long snout opening wide, baring rows of sharp, pointy teeth at them.

"<A demonic-force barrier... Satan! Are you Satan?!>"

"...Huh?"

The voice, from deep inside his throat, was only understandable to Maou.

"<I was searching for you, Satan! That traitor Camuinica abandoned his duties and attempted to kill me! He must pay!>"

"M-me? Camui… What?"

"<Satan, Camuinica is colluding with the warrior Legoon! You must shore up your defenses! Where is Camuinica? Has he returned yet?!>"

"Does this demon have some business with you, Maou? I think the gator is looking at us."

"Umm… He's speaking demonic, yeah, but I'm not sure what he's talking about. Who was Camuinica again? That name sounds familiar…"

But as Amane and Maou gave each other confused glances, they heard a weak voice behind them.

"C-Camuinica…is my father…*peep*…"

They whirled around to find a black chicken in the arms of Urushihara, the fallen angel spreading his wings wide to stay aloft and looking like he'd rather be anywhere else.

"Camio?!"

"<Ah! Camuinica! There you are!!>"

The alligator beneath them suddenly let out a roar of rage.

"<How dare you hide yourself all this time! Satan! That is a traitor before you!>"

"Uh, Camio, I'm assuming that when he says 'Satan,' he's not talking about me, right?"

"Indeed, my liege. He speaks of Satan, the original Devil Overlord—in other words, the angel Satanael. It would also appear he has mistaken me for my father."

"<Camuinica! I have gathered more demonic force in this land, and now I shall use it to send you to the afterlife! Prepare to die!>"

"Whoa, Maou, I think he's gonna breathe something at us!" Amane warned. "I *really* don't like how he's acting!"

"He's not that powerful. Here, get behind me, everyone—"

"<Die!!>"

"Whoa?!"

As Amane predicted, the alligator emitted some kind of energy beam from his mouth, aimed straight at the group. The attack was, fortunately, nothing worth losing sleep over. Maou had torn out of his apartment without replenishing his demonic energy at all, but one lift of his arm was still enough to make it vanish. But that wasn't the problem.

"<Nh...nhhh...>"

The change was dramatic. The beam closed itself off, like turning a spigot—and like a deflated balloon, the alligator's body started to shrink.

"<Argh... Gah...>"

In a few short seconds, the gigantic reptile had shrunk down to a somewhat plus-sized lizard.

"What was that?"

"It is the same behavior seen in my own species, sir," Camio said. "His clan, the Lenbrellebelve, shrink in size whenever faced with great danger."

"Lenbrellebelve?" exclaimed Urushihara. "Didn't the Devil Overlord keep one of those?"

"You knew about that, Lucifer? Indeed, this is the lone survivor of the Lenbrellebelve species. Its final chieftain."

"<Arghh... Camui...nica...>"

The exhausted lizard flipped on its back, limbs spread wide. They could tell it was alive, given the way its throat rhythmically breathed in and out, but that wasn't where their attention was focused.

"What's that on the guy's throat?"

"I believe, Your Demonic Highness, that is the Astral Gem."

"...Huh?"

Urushihara scowled. "I shoulda guessed."

"Yes," Camio said in a weak but shrill voice that seemed to thunder in Maou's ears, "the jewel embedded in the body of Kinanna, chief of the Lenbrellebelve, is likely the final relic we seek."

THE
HERO
REVEALS
DEEP
ANXIETIES
ABOUT
THE
FUTURE

The morning after an enormous cryptid haunted Yoyogi Park, Room 201 of Villa Rosa Sasazuka enjoyed its largest audience in quite some time. The whole gang was there—Maou, Ashiya, Emi, Chiho, Suzuno, Amane, Laila, and even Villa Rosa landlord Miki Shiba. Alas Ramus, Acieth, and Erone were down in Room 101 watching TV with Nord, just in case their presence set off the lizard. Urushihara, meanwhile, was holed up inside the closet, given the changes to his hair color (and everything else) whenever Shiba came near him.

Maou, having gotten used to enjoying this room all by himself, frowned a bit at the sight. But that didn't matter right now. Instead, all eyes were focused on a single point in the room.

"Mr. Maou?"

It was Shiba who spoke first, looking uncharacteristically concerned.

"You *do* know that your lease forbids pets, don't you?"

"They're not pets. Technically. Cut me some slack."

That's what you bring up first? thought everyone else, although they were too cowed to say it.

"I am sorry," the crestfallen Camio said in his box. "If only I weren't in this sad state of affairs..."

"No, no, my liege," Ashiya said, giving the chicken a reassuring pat on the back. "If anything, Lord Camio, your normal form would present more problems for us here in Japan than this one."

But everyone else was focused on the cage on the table, a cage crafted from holy energy that currently had a sleeping lizard curled up inside—a mere echo of the crocodilian monster of Yoyogi Park that Maou and Amane had seen last night.

✳

Once the lizard demon pulled that shrinking act at the park, Amane and Maou remained up in the air, trying to figure out how to take him home with them without attracting attention. They ultimately decided to use Maou's force to magically lift the inert, unresponsive creature up to them.

"My liege, you mustn't!"

Camio's pleading made Maou stop, but a little demonic force still launched itself off from his fingers. The effect was stark: In an instant, the lizard blew up to the size of a juvenile alligator. It didn't wake it up, but the experiment proved that the monster had an uncanny ability to soak in demonic force.

"Maybe I can step in?"

Amane curled a finger upward. This time, the alligator's body floated up without further incident.

"I can't wait to see the tweets about this tomorrow. A cryptid appears in Yoyogi Park, only to die and ascend to heaven! And oh, all the witnesses!"

She seemed to be almost looking forward to it. Maou wasn't. And the world didn't even wait until tomorrow—by the time they got back home, Urushihara had tabs open of videos of the alligator lumbering around, the moment of the explosion, even the little guy bobbing around in the air before Amane hefted him into the air.

"I went through all the media I could find, but I didn't see any that showed us, at least, so don't worry about that. You can see a couple of vaguely human silhouettes in one or two of them, though. I guess that guy must've absorbed the demon-energy barrier you put up."

"And you want me to 'not worry' about that? It sounds like I should worry about it a *lot*, actually!"

A tired-looking Maou placed a call to Emi. "We took care of everything, but now we got some other crap to deal with. You mind coming here to the apartment ASAP?" he asked.

"Sure, but what happened?"

"I know this isn't really your wheelhouse, but I got no one else to turn to. Suzuno and Emeralda are in Ente Isla, and I dunno if I can wait forty minutes for them to get back here."

"What about Chiho? Should I take her along?"

"No, that might make things worse. I'm here now with Urushihara, actually, but our hands are kind of tied at the moment. I'm being forced to ask Amane to take care of things."

"Okay. I'll be right there. All right, Chiho, I need to—"

Maou could hear her say something to Chiho before cutting the call off. He flipped his phone shut, then stared at it for a moment. "You know," he muttered to himself, "Emi really isn't *that* much of an obstacle these days, is she…?"

✻

"So?"

It was Suzuno who spoke next, looking and sounding very peeved.

"Are you saying this *reptile* destroyed the backyard?"

"Um, pretty much."

"What happened? Because depending on the answer to that, I *will* exact penance from you."

Suzuno could likely be forgiven for her bad mood. The situation out back behind the Villa Rosa Sasazuka building wasn't as bad as what they saw in Yoyogi Pak earlier, but there was still a deep gouge in the ground, and the concrete-block wall surrounding it was nearly collapsing in places. There used to be a nice little vegetable

garden back there, the product of careful work on Suzuno's part, but now it was just a big clump of distressed-looking soil.

"We can't afford to let this guy taste any demonic energy at all," Urushihara explained. "We didn't know that at first, so when he woke up in here, he started freaking out. Sorry about that."

"Yeah, I don't even want to think about what'd happen if I still had that demonic force stored in my closet. We didn't think the little guy would be such a menace, so… My bad."

There was enough force in the closet to refill Maou's demonic force to maximum, even in his full demon form. If a lizard *that* hungry for it chanced upon that stash and absorbed it, they'd have a lot more than a ruined vegetable garden on their hands. Urushihara's banishing of the demon outside to secure more closet space for himself wound up saving them all by the narrowest of margins. For now, that force was being kept under careful guard at Shiba's house.

"This was kind of my fault, too," Amane added, looking a lot more despondent than usual. "It was totally out of control, and after we saw what he did in Yoyogi Park, I threw him out to the backyard before he could knock the whole apartment building down. I didn't know you had a garden back there… Sorry."

"Well…in that case…"

She sounded so apologetic—not at all her usual freewheeling self—that Suzuno couldn't chide her that much. Besides, while she did set up the garden herself, she left the upkeep to Urushihara the majority of the time, and it was still new. Apart from the monetary loss, there wasn't much real damage done.

"So what *is* this guy, then? If that stone on his neck is the Astral Gem, does that make this demon a relic of the Devil Overlord's?"

Under bright light like this, it was clear that the stone buried in his throat was an integral part of its body, easily mistakable as a cousin of the horns, fangs, and claws that'd naturally grow on it.

"I really wish this demon wasn't alive like this, but maybe you're right. Look." Laila pointed at the lizard's neck.

His body was covered in dark reddish-brown scales, but his neck, and the area around the stone, exhibited a dazzling array of colors, sparkling in the natural sunlight like a rainbow necklace. It almost seemed too elegant of a touch for the rugged lizard trying to sleep.

"I thought," Urushihara said from behind the closet door, "the Astral Gem was supposed to be on the Lenbrellebelve's collar. That *kind* of looks like a collar, doesn't it?"

"I wish it wasn't," Emi retorted, "in a lot of ways. Did Satanael do this?"

"I'm sorry," said Laila, "I don't know. I didn't hear any details about the relics."

Laila, Emi's mother and someone around back when Satanael was still alive, was just as confused as the rest of them as she watched the lizard.

"So if this stone's the Astral Gem," a still-huffy Suzuno said, "what now? Are we going to rip it out of his throat? I imagine that would kill him."

"Assuming that is even possible," Ashiya reminded her. "Because if you put what Amane and Lord Camio said together, this is no regular demon. In case you forgot, Lord Camio is an arch-demon so powerful that Barbariccia and other Malebranche chieftains recognize him as my liege's representative in the demon realms. Having a demon strong enough to give both him and an angel an even fight at the same time, running free in the demon realms like it apparently was... It is certainly a shock."

It turned out that the great majority of Camio's injuries were caused by this lizard—or to be exact, the Lenbrellebelve chief, Kinanna. In fact, it was likely Kinanna who threw Camael's spear into Chiho's room, after misidentifying Camio as his foe. If both he and Camio came to Japan at the same time, it was a miracle that Kinanna had remained undetected for as long as he had.

"As you saw," Camio explained, "this Kinanna knows the name of Camuinica, my father. When I approached him to discuss the possible handover of the Astral Gem, he accused me of being Camuinica—and right then, that angel leaped toward Kinanna, trying to kill him for the same purpose. So he fought both of us back."

"There's nothing good about Camael, is there?" Laila muttered. Emi internally agreed with her.

"And as for why he grew so big in the park... Devil King, Alciel, that was likely your fault."

"Huh?" "What?"

"That's about where you guys first fell into Japan at, isn't it?" Emi accused. "The demonic force that leaked out of your bodies here, after your final battle with me... It's still lurking around, and now it's causing us some serious trouble."

"Wh-what do you mean?" Maou protested. Instead of answering him, Emi turned to Kinanna.

"Bell does have a point," the Hero went on. "If we try to take the stone out of that thing when it's so clearly a part of his body, no way he's going to survive that. Are you okay with that? Because...I kind of had a traumatic moment like that once, and I really don't want to kill the lizard if I can avoid it."

"Ah, yes," Suzuno whispered to herself. "There *was* that..."

"Well, yeah," Maou added, "I don't wanna kill him, either. That's just wrong."

Tiny lizard or not, this was a full-fledged demon. The Astral Gem was a must if Maou wanted to reach his goals and Ente Isla wanted lasting peace. But was it worth taking the life of this demon? Nobody was expecting to be asked to weigh the value of someone's life like this. It made the air heavy around the apartment. Was it right to sacrifice a single life for the sake of many? It was a common question, but one that nobody could ever really answer, and now the strongest of humans and demons were seated together in silence, pondering it.

"Um, I have a question."

It was Chiho who broke that silence, sitting toward the rear of the room and keeping quiet until now.

"Is that stone in his throat *really* the Astral Gem?"

""""Huh?"""""

Everyone stared at her like she had gone mad. She realized her point was being misunderstood.

"Um, you're all saying that the stone in, uh, 'Kinanna'? His neck? …is the Astral Gem, but are you sure about that?"

"Sure…um, aren't we?" Maou was about to brush the thought away, only to realize he couldn't, exactly. He took another glance at Kinanna's throat. "I mean, it looks that way. Like, the colors and the shape and its appearance."

"But doesn't the stone go up and down in size with Kinanna? Because if *that's* the Astral Gem, then it's really small."

"Oh…"

Maou thoughtfully nodded. She had a point.

"I mean, I've only seen one other relic, but this just seems way too small compared to the Spear. I'm sure it's super-powerful no matter what size it is, but I just think, you know, we should stop talking about killing him or pulling it out of him until we're really sure that's the Astral Gem."

The room fell silent again, this time for different reasons.

"…What do you think of that, Camio? Because you were pretty confident it was the Astral Gem last night."

"The legends speak of Kinanna…or *peep*, or the Lenbrellebelve serving as guardians of the Gem. And we have found nothing else that could possibly *peep* the Gem besides this."

Camio seemed to be losing his confidence as well.

"Right," Amane said. "We'll have to wait for him to wake up… but depending on how that goes, we might have more than a ruined garden to think about. Can we do something about that hunk of demonic force you're storing, Maou? Because if he sucks all *that* up, he's gonna turn into the kind of lizard that smashes up Tokyo Tower and stomps all over government buildings."

The tiny bit of telekinetic magic Maou tapped to lift his body up was enough to turn Kinanna into a large, vicious, garden-destroying monster. If that demon swallowed up a crystal of magic powerful enough to fully recharge Maou or Ashiya, it was hard to imagine what the results could be.

"Uh, Ashiya, you think you could maybe ferry that back to Ente Isla? Like, right now?"

"Yes, my liege. I have my concerns about leaving such a large store of energy over *there* as well, but we have little choice. I have to say, I was not expecting an obstacle like *this* right at the end of our search. I will tell the other leaders there about this, but I imagine we will need to regroup and reposition our strategy. My liege, what is your work schedule looking like?"

"I start in the afternoon today, so I still got some time. Tomorrow I'm there pretty much all day, so I can't help you then."

Amane rolled her eyes at Maou. "You're going to *work* right now? Can't you take time off? This is kind of urgent."

The statement made nearly everyone there—Maou, Emi, Chiho, Ashiya, Urushihara, and Suzuno—realize they all assumed they'd have to figure something out with Camio and Kinanna while Maou was at work.

"His Demonic Highness is at a crucial point in his career, Amane."

That was why Ashiya, who didn't know better, was the first to reply to Amane, trying to offer an excuse to her.

"My liege is in the middle of managerial training. I believe his final interview and approval is coming up soon, but if he takes time off suddenly at such a vital moment, there is no telling how that may affect his evaluation."

"...!"

"...Oh."

"..."

Ashiya was so busy addressing Amane that he didn't see the reactions from Maou, Urushihara, or Emi. Chiho and Suzuno noticed them instead. It made their eyebrows dart up a little.

"Regardless, Urushihara, I want you to guard Room 201 like before," Ashiya said. "If something happens, take care of it. We will talk about tomorrow onward later on. Do you work today, too, Emilia?"

"...No. Chiho has today off, so I do, too."

"Ah. In that case, you may help keep Ms. Sasaki safe should worse come to worst. And you, Bell...?"

"...I have to return to Ente Isla today as well, but I have some time to work with. I need to reinforce the cage we have Kinanna in. You can return ahead of me."

The lizard's cage naturally couldn't be made of demonic energy, so Emi cast a couple of unfamiliar-to-her spells to construct it. But she was no expert, so it was left to Suzuno to complete the job.

"Very well. For now, it is crucial that we leave no demonic force around for Kinanna to absorb. Lucifer, my liege, do you have enough reserve left in you?"

"...Sure."

"Yeah, dude, it's not like that guy can suck it out of our bodies."

"Then I will leave at once. Ms. Shiba, I apologize for always causing you trouble, but I promise we will make up for it at a later date. For now, I hope you will be lenient with Kinanna here."

"No, no," the landlord cheerfully replied, "no need to hurry."

With their farewells taken care of, Ashiya joined Shiba to pick up the magic crystal at her house, Laila standing up to join them.

"I better go back, too. I need to check with Gabriel about how heaven's reacting to the relics. Take care of your father for me, Emilia."

"Yeah. All right."

Mother and daughter waved at each other, the wall separating them quite a bit lower than it used to be.

Ten or so minutes later, the room was a little emptier than before, occupied by Maou, Chiho, Emi, Suzuno, Urushihara (now freed from his closet exile), Camio, and Kinanna.

"Uh, why're you looking at me?" Maou asked, unable to hold eye contact with the female members of the audience. "Because I think Urushihara and I can handle things for today, but..."

Chiho, Emi, and Suzuno didn't move a muscle. Seeing this, Maou sighed.

"All right. I give up. I told Urushihara last night, but—I got rejected for a managerial position."

"What...?"

"Ah, was that what happened?"

"I kind of had a suspicion, yeah."

"Wait. Chi and Suzuno didn't know?"

Chiho looked honestly surprised, at a loss for words, and it seemed to be news to Suzuno as well. It wasn't at all what Maou expected.

"I mean," Chiho nervously ventured, "you've been acting a little different since yesterday..."

Suzuno averted her eyes. "It did seem like you were trying to hide something from Alciel, yes... But you have yet to break the news to him?"

"I can't bring myself to...or maybe I feel sorry for him...or I just feel pathetic about it. Lots of stuff."

He had always been a faithful Great Demon General, but ever since they came to Japan, Ashiya had been an anchor for everything Maou did, willing to sacrifice almost everything for the sake of his lord's dreams. And now there was no reward Maou could offer him.

In a way, Ashiya was taking command in Ente Isla like he had in years past, overseeing field operations in a position roughly similar to Camio's—all because Maou had his own "work" to attend to. But when it came time to storm heaven, he would doubtlessly leave the captain's chair to Maou.

"I know he's gonna find out anyway," he explained. "I just thought, maybe, instead of telling him when all this crazy stuff is going on, I could apologize about it once things settle down."

"Once things settle down *when*?" Emi groused.

Maou gave her a vague smile. "...Good question."

He knew what the woman meant. Chiho, Suzuno, and Urushihara all knew what impact Maou's failing to get salaried at MgRonald would have on his relationship with her.

"Your Demonic Highness," Camio calmly stated, "things rarely work out exactly as one plans them. We, too, faced many trials and tribulations of our own, on our mission to conquer and unite the demon realms. Your actions in battle were so brazen, so unheard-of, that I cannot count the number of times I expected death to take me, *churrr.*"

He probably had no idea what MgRonald was, much less what

being a manager of one entailed. But this old fighter understood well enough that his general had faced a punishing trial and was found wanting.

"*Ba-kluk.* But the Devil King I know would never give up after such a setback. You did not flee to this world following Emilia the Hero's victory simply because you valued your own life too much to lose it, *peep.*"

"Can you not say that when the Hero's right here, please?"

Emi couldn't help but chuckle. Camio was starting to sound like an old man admonishing his grandson. But the sight of her loosening up helped ease the stress in the minds of Chiho, Suzuno, and Urushihara as well.

"Well, I don't even *know* about that. When Emi and I were duking it out, it was intense. Even more than it was against Ashiya. I had my hands totally full."

"…" "!"

Urushihara and Chiho knew what he meant by that. Emi and Suzuno let it slide.

"*Ba-kluk.* But even if the damage to your side grew over time, the Devil King I know always found ingenious measures to turn the tables and secure victory. So take heart. To you, my liege, the human race barely even registers as an enemy, *peep.*"

Nobody could say Camio was wrong. Not too long ago, Emi and Suzuno would've reflexively self-identified as his enemy. Now they stayed silent.

"For now, carry on with your regular efforts. Lucifer and I are keeping watch over Kinanna. And Emilia the Hero, Chiho Sasaki, and Crestia Bell… One moment— *Peep?!*"

"C-Camio?!"

He had tried to get out of the box by himself, only to lose his balance on the lip and crash to the floor. Chiho helped him up, and once he was back on his feet, he opened a wing and bowed deeply to the three women, just as he did at Ohguro-ya back in the summer.

"I am sure all of you have your grudges. Someday, we demons may clash swords with you humans yet again. But for now, for the sake of all who live and breathe on Ente Isla, I want everyone to help my lord through his hardships. This, I humbly ask of you...*churrr.*"

"C-Camio!" a flustered Chiho replied. "Lift your head back up! I've always been on Maou's side!"

The thoroughly chastened Maou didn't speak. Not even Camio's interspersed peeping could provide relief from the hard truth. Maou's representative from the demon realms, someone with no great attachment to Japan, had just bowed his head to humans. All he knew was that his lord, Satan, the Devil King, was faced with adversity, and that drove him to bow to his previous enemies.

"Lift your face, good Sir Camio."

Suzuno took his wing. It seemed so natural of her that neither Maou, nor Emi, nor Chiho, nor Urushihara realized the historical importance of the moment. For the first time, Suzuno had addressed a demon with heartfelt respect.

"Humans and demons are enemies. But on the surface at least, Satan, the Devil King, is my military superior, and beyond that, my neighbor. On Earth, we say that a friend in need is a friend indeed. I cannot say what will happen after our conquest of heaven, but for now, Camio, I want to respect your innermost feelings."

"I most *peep*ly thank you," the emotionally overcome Camio said.

Urushihara, gauging this, turned toward the others. "...Well?"

"I'm not getting caught up in this," Emi stated.

"No?" He grinned. "And here I thought you would."

"I am the Devil King's enemy. Through and through."

"Huh. Neat."

"I wasn't expecting any of that from you anyway. If you started sympathizing with *me*, I'd get utterly depressed."

Urushihara and Maou had both nodded at her cold reaction. It was, if nothing else, in character.

Emi responded by lifting her eyebrows a little. "Right? This makes things easier for you, too, doesn't it? So I'm fine with it."

"""..."""

The two men gave her deer-in-headlights looks, while Chiho gave her a half-exasperated, half-impressed grin, and Suzuno just shrugged her disapproval. And Camio, watching it, lifted up the edges of his beak in a smile that none of the humans could have detected. Adramelech and Malacoda were gone, but now, Satan was gifted with close companions who were every bit their equals. Nothing could have made Camio more elated to see.

"But still," Maou said, voice a little shaky as he attempted to refocus the conversation, "either way, we got a mountain of problems to deal with. In Ente Isla and in Japan. My managerial bid came and went, and there's no point worrying about it now. But you two…"

"What?"

"Yes?"

"Emi, Chiho, I think I'm gonna have a lot of crap to deal with, as soon as today. I would've preferred if Kisaki could've told you herself, but you two are kind of special exceptions to me, so I'll tell you while I still can."

The revelation he had for them made Emi and Chiho tense up, for two different reasons. It even made Suzuno stare blankly at him.

"Ms. Kisaki's going to be transferred at the start of the fiscal year. She's gonna be leaving Hatagaya Station."

✳

"Is it me, or are things a lot quieter across the street?"

Maou couldn't help but notice the lack of activity at the Sentucky Fried Chicken facing MgRonald as he parked Dullahan II at the bike rack.

What would its manager, Mitsuki Sarue—Sariel the archangel—do once he found out Kisaki would be moving on? Most likely, Maou reasoned, he would follow her. His passion and his knack for turning it into unwanted action were both intense. If the heavens were as dull and listless as Gabriel described them, it was a miracle he had retained such a stultifying and pushy attitude for so many eons. But Kisaki would have an HQ office job. If Sariel wanted to remain near her, he'd have to find a way to get into MgRonald, just as he did with Sentucky in the past.

The morning crew at MgRonald must have heard the news by now. *I'll need to share some info with them*, Maou thought as he went through the employee entrance, *and we'll need to form a strategy to deal with Sarue's inevitable storming of the dining room.*

When he went in, he felt it.

"What's this...feeling in the air...?"

It was like a heavy weight suddenly pressed upon his shoulders. He looked around, surprised. Akiko Ohki, noticing him, ran up.

"Ah! Maou! Over there!"

"What?"

Akiko pointed at what appeared, at first, to be a whirling coil of darkness. Maou focused on it. It revealed a single customer, seated at the far end of the table space. Just a single customer, but...

"Why is he here? And so worked up already?!"

It was indeed Mitsuki Sarue, and he was gaunt, haggard—a completely different person from the last time they'd spoken. His face resembled a weathered sheet of paper, liable to break apart into little pieces at the slightest prodding. If you let your eyes off of him for a moment, he looked ready to sink through the floor and into the underworld, perhaps taking an unlucky soul or two with him.

"So you knew about Ms. Kisaki getting transferred, Maou?"

That had to be it. Akiko and the crew would know, of course, but how had Sariel sniffed it out so quickly? Did he really know? But if not, what else would make him so depressed?

"Is Ms. Kisaki in here?"

"She came in to tell everyone but then went to the home office for a managerial meeting. She said she'd be back around three or so. But um, about Mr. Sarue..."

What Maou heard next made him doubt his ears.

"She *told* him?!"

"*Rrwwww!*"

A groan like the wailing of the dead welled up from the darkness in the corner. Maou and Akiko ignored it.

"I was so surprised, too! But I guess she had a reason to... Like, she said she wanted to do it herself, but she told one of the Sentucky crewmembers instead of telling him directly. She did it that way because there's this part-timer who apparently knows how to handle Sarue really well, so that's probably how he found out."

Someone knows how to handle Sarue? They must have a heart of iron. Maou never heard of the person before, but if they had an employee who could navigate Sariel and live to tell the tale, he really wanted to chat sometime.

"Ms. Kisaki said it's better to just lay down the law with him early on instead of having him explode afterward, but..."

"'Laying down the law' could kill him. If anything goes wrong with this..."

"Yeah. She gave the crew permission to keep their phones on them at all times for today. The office phone is kind of far away, you know, if...stuff happens."

It was martial law at MgRonald. Nobody could predict what kind of bizarre, perhaps criminal behavior Sarue would engage in once he learned the truth. But in a way, Maou was surprised. If Kisaki was really leaving, he assumed Sarue would be constantly nagging everyone related to her, hoping for some kind of an in. But if he was acting all shocked like this, it at least meant he was in the process of parsing his new normal—a reality where he'd have to be away from Kisaki. (Not that they were "close," exactly, but still.)

For the time being, it was safe for the crew to assume that the chair in the corner would not be available to other customers the rest of the day. Even if Sarue left, the residual accursed miasma surrounding him might put a hex on whoever sat there next.

"Um, okay. Let me clock in first, and then we'll talk."

"Oh, sorry. But yeah, he's been in here for almost two hours without even lifting a finger, so I think we're good, but..."

He's already been like that for two hours? The sheer devotion struck Maou as simply ridiculous. So he changed the subject, his voice casual.

"By the way, Aki, they turned me down for a manager job."

Akiko's eyes widened in surprise. "What? They did?! If they turned *you* down, who would they possibly say yes to?!"

"I dunno. Nobody else I interacted with during the testing got accepted."

Come to think of it, Ms. Kusuda, the woman who'd met Maou during the seminar and given him chocolate for Valentine's Day, had been crossed off at the third round of testing. Nitta, the guy who'd tried to get a party going for the whole crew, was rejected in the final interview, along with Maou. He had chatted with a number of other applicants during the process, but he wasn't friendly enough with any of them to ask how things had turned out for them afterward.

"Wow... I mean, really...? Now *I'm* starting to worry."

"What for?"

"I'm gonna graduate from college next year, so I need to start looking for a full-time job, like Kota. But really, I thought the restaurant business was gonna be easier than this. I figured it'd be a breeze as long as I wasn't too picky...but if you think about it, there's no way I could perform like Ms. Kisaki. I feel kind of stupid now, you know? But...wow, they'd reject someone as top-performing as *you*?"

"I guess. They didn't tell me why or anything. So I'm gonna be working here like normal past March, after all."

"Oh. Well, if you aren't leaving, then no offense, but that's great for us, so..." Akiko sighed. "When I didn't get into college the first time around and took a year off to study, my parents got insanely strict with me. And I know it was my fault and stuff, but... Man, if I have to repeat a year or can't find a job, my mother's totally gonna kill me. How can *I* be more like Kisaki, I wonder...?"

"Nobody can be totally like her. Hey, I gotta change real quick, okay?"

"Ahh, sorry. I'll leave you alone. But don't feel too down, okay? The seniors in my classes told me to expect an avalanche of rejection letters, so..."

Akiko, who had unconsciously followed Maou into the staff room, excused herself.

"Finding steady work's hard for everyone, I guess. I wonder if Kota's having a hard time...?"

Maou recalled Kotaro Nakayama, another MgRonald long-termer

who'd quit a short while ago. College students in Japan generally joined the work-recruitment process at the end of their junior year, in the winter and spring, and Kotaro left MgRonald so he could focus on it. Maou knew it was an arduous process, one in which a student may file applications with dozens, even hundreds of firms.

"I'm sure Kota would laugh at me if he saw me all depressed about this. That or yell at me."

Maou had been rejected by exactly one company. Why was he so confident, so self-assured, that he'd get his shot with the exact job he wanted and nail it on the first try? Up until now, that kind of luck almost never happened to him. Being rejected wasn't exactly fun, but the shock had subsided quite a bit. There was no rule prohibiting him from applying again, and there were a million companies besides MgRonald out there.

Compared to Akiko's or Kawata's or Kotaro's, Maou's résumé—consisting of no college education and a long stream of part-time jobs—didn't do him many favors. But Maou almost never started something with a decisive advantage. He usually faced adversity the whole way; none of it could be described as smooth sailing, at least not until he had almost finished conquering the demon realms.

"I've really gotten soft, haven't I? If I can't power my way through something, it really beats on me mentally."

Whether conquering the demon realms or invading Ente Isla, in the end, it mostly came down to forcing his will on others with his powers. Applying for a managerial post was another story. It involved trying to win someone's trust through nothing but words and actions.

"I hope I can be patient with this."

Only with that pep talk did Maou find it in him to assume the guise of Sadao Maou, A-class MgRonald crewmember.

No matter what Urushihara said, Maou felt—for wholly different reasons from before—that working his way up in human society would play a vital role in his future as the Devil King. He could only reveal why to a select few people, but not long from now, he was positive the effort would pay off. He had talked about it with Ashiya many times before; he'd never mentioned it to Urushihara, since he was so chatty and inconsiderate that there was no telling when he'd blab about it. Emi, Suzuno, and Emeralda in particular couldn't be let in on it until there was no turning back.

That was why, for now, he had to give everything he could to his work.

"Right. First, let's deal with Sariel. Next I gotta reinspect all the spots I didn't get around to yesterday, and then..."

He pulled his visor down a little and opened the staff room door. Sariel—the first thing to "deal with"—was still in the corner, wavering in the air like a ghoul from some occult hot spot. Striking up a conversation would be ill-advised; until he did something on his own volition, it was better to let sleeping dogs lie.

Things proceeded smoothly all morning, until the AM crew left after the lunch rush. Everyone was thoroughly ignoring the ghoul in the corner; the regulars took one look at him and assumed he did something to piss off Kisaki yet again. But then, around two PM, when Maou happened to be running downstairs from the café space:

"Are you still feeling sorry for yourself in here?! Hurry up and get back to work already! Do you want me to tell Ms. Tanaka about this?! Ms. Kisaki's never gonna talk to you again!"

It was a loud, confident-looking woman in a Sentucky uniform. Maou stared wide-eyed at her; she gave him a nod, stepped up to the ghoul, and pulled him away from the darkness.

"And can you *please* stop using that chair long after you're done eating? You're embarrassing me!"

The wraith let the young woman drag him by the collar, along the floor and toward Maou.

"Are you Mr. Maou, the shift supervisor?"

"Yes ma'am..."

"I apologize that Sarue's being such an annoyance to you. My name's Kanako Furuya, and I'm a shift supervisor at Sentucky across the street."

Her eyes, framed by her neatly cut short hair, left an immediate impression. She was clearly strong-willed—and she had to be, or else she wouldn't be manhandling the worn-out husk of Sariel with a single hand. In terms of her purification skills, and in terms of being broad-hearted enough to accept someone with Sariel's personality in her life, she had a bright future ahead as a cleric in Ente Isla's Church bureaucracy.

"Ms. Kisaki told me about her transfer, and I tried to give him the news as easy as I could, but I guess it was just too much of a shock for the man… I apologize for having him occupy your dining space for so long."

"N-no, um, Mr. Sarue is a valued customer of ours…"

"Well, I appreciate you saying that. We all do."

Furuya looked exasperated but not at all exhausted. A very strong woman, no doubt. Otherwise, she'd never be able to work under such a moody manager.

"Whew! Finally, Kana to the rescue!"

Akiko, running up to Maou, breathed a sigh of relief.

"Oh, hello, Ms. Ohki. I'm sorry I have to keep fetching my good-for-nothing manager."

"It's all right. We're all used to it by now!"

Akiko and Furuya must have known each other. They said their good-byes, Akiko giving her a flurry of polite bows as she dragged her boss off.

"Well," Akiko said when Maou asked about their connection, "Kawacchi and I were run pretty ragged during Valentine's Day, and she was kind of like our war buddy in the trenches."

On Valentine's, Maou had been out in managerial training, and Chiho had been too preoccupied with the zirga over on Ente Isla to pay much attention to her work. Sariel was undoubtedly acting like a maniac on that day, fully expecting Kisaki to give him chocolate.

"You know, I actually didn't hear much about how that day turned out. Anything rough?"

"I was expecting the worst, kinda, but Kisaki did her duty and gave Sarue a little bit of chocolate out of duty's sake, so it was all good."

"Kisaki gave Sariel chocolate?!"

It surprised Maou so much that he accidentally used Sarue's real name, but he spoke it so fast that Akiko failed to notice.

"Ha-ha-ha! Chiho had the same reaction. I could hardly believe it myself!" Akiko looked toward the entrance Kanako just dragged Sariel through and snickered. "I have no idea what kind of unlucky star Sarue was born under, you know? Just a bit ago, he was going around like a Buddhist priest who found enlightenment or something, and now it's like he's a vengeful spirit from hell."

Maou could imagine how the sugary gift would be like achieving nirvana for Sariel. But an angel going from nirvana to the deepest pits of hell was quite a transformation. Which hell that would be—Earth's or somewhere else's—was a topic up for debate, however.

"What a pain," he blurted out.

"Yeah, but at least Kana came to pick him up. Let me cleanse the evil spirits real quick."

Akiko took up a duster and some alcohol to clean Sariel's table. Right when she was about wrapped up, Kisaki emerged from the staff room, warily eyeing the dining space.

"Did he show up? Or is he gone already?"

"Good afternoon, Ms. Kisaki!"

"Hey there, Marko. Anything happen here?"

Maou didn't know if Kisaki could sense the undead or not, but she must have had an inkling, at least. She gave Sariel's seat a perplexed look, then turned back to him.

"All clear, then?"

"...Yes."

He didn't need to have Kisaki spell out her intent. If anything, he felt a little awkward about replying. It implied that she knew a lot more about Kisaki than he intended to let on.

"Well, good job, Marko. I was expecting it to take longer, but you put your foot down, huh?"

"We have to, or else we'll never get anywhere with him."

"No, you sure won't. You're right." Kisaki cracked her neck, looking fatigued as she surveyed the space. "With most things in this world, if you keep sweating the small stuff, you'll never get anywhere... Sorry to ask you again, but you wanna hang out for a quick dinner again after work today?"

"Sure, I'd be—"

He'd be happy to, but then his memory reminded him of something. He had some serious issues left unresolved at home. If anything, he really needed to get over there early this evening.

"...Oh, um, I'm sorry, but I need to be home ASAP tonight."

"Oh? Sure, that's fine. It's nothing urgent anyway. Next time! But if Sarue was in here, how're our afternoon sales?"

Kisaki sprang right back into business mode—but Maou couldn't begin to guess why Kisaki was inviting him out after work two days in a row. His mind pondered it for a while after, distracting him from work. After all, the next time he could accept that invite—or any invite, really—depended on the lizard in his apartment.

✳

"Kind of dark out, huh?"

The sky, as seen out the front windows from inside the shuttered dining space, did indeed look unusually dark. It couldn't have been Sariel turning Sentucky across the street into an undead house of horrors, but when Maou went outside, he found the night sky starless and the temperature unseasonably cold.

"I guess we'll still see some cold nights for a while, huh? Better head right home after I wrap— *Aaaahhhhhh?!*"

As he shut off the automatic doors and stepped out to take all the outdoor displays in, Maou was spooked by a dark presence crouching in the shadows.

"What is it, Marko?!" Kisaki shouted from inside.

"Um, n-nothing! I just tripped on something!"

"Oh! Well, be careful!"

"Okay! ... *What* are you doing down there?"

Maou was still in a cold sweat as he bent down and spoke to the presence.

"...I'm cold."

"Yeah, I bet. You still need a coat if you go out in Tokyo in March. How long have you been there?"

It was Sariel, of course, in his street clothes and on his knees in front of a row of plants by the MgRonald entrance.

"I finished closing just now, and um, the moment I left Sentucky, my legs gave out on me."

At least he kept up with his work duties, Maou thought.

"Wow. I guess you'll just have to freeze to death within the hour, then." His gaze narrowed pointedly. "You weren't planning to ambush Ms. Kisaki, were you?"

"Of course not. If I wanted to ambush her, I'd stake out the staff entrance."

He may have been rotten to the core, but he was still coolheaded enough to just barely avoid committing any crimes. Maou wondered how he did it.

"I finished the workday in utter despair. When I left, the lights of MgRonald looked so warm and inviting. The happy times I've spent here floated to my mind before disappearing, so fleeting...and then they would come back, again and again. And as I marveled at this, I found myself unable to move an inch."

"Can you just go home, please? I know you live close to here. If you freeze to death in front of our entrance, that goes *way* past just annoying all of us, y'know."

Sariel was starting to sound like the fairy-tale Little Match Girl. Giving him attention would delay his store-closing duties. Thus, Maou paid him no further mind, making sure to lock the automatic doors once he was back outside.

"Ahh... God...heaven...Earth mother... Whatever should I do...?"

Maou put his hands to his ears, shutting out the weak whisper leaking through just before the doors shut for good.

"…Was that Sarue out there?" Kisaki asked with a grin.

"Yeah. He was going on like the Little Match Girl."

"Oh. Well, if he's gonna freeze to death, can you tell him to do it somewhere else?"

Hans Christian Andersen would likely be aghast, but the two of them continued their work without further comment on Sariel. When they left through the back door, all that greeted them were the sights of the city at night. The presence was gone from the front as well; he must have left in the last ten or fifteen minutes.

Once she was sure Sarue was gone, Kisaki gave Maou a malcontented sniff.

"Hmph. You know, I always thought he was a weak man."

"Pardon?"

"Ah, never mind. Good work today. See you later."

"Um, sure. You too."

So Kisaki headed home, not looking particularly scared of Sarue or even particularly tired after a full day of work. Maou watched her for a moment…and then it struck him. As long as he didn't get violent, Sariel really didn't matter. He really *did* need to get home fast, or else he'd put unneeded stress on Urushihara and Camio—and most importantly of all, perhaps even anger their landlord.

Hopping on Dullahan II, Maou pedaled as fast as he could back to the apartment. But when he raced up the stairs and opened the door to Room 201, he just stood there blankly.

"What in the…hell…?"

It was no longer the room he had left that morning.

The morning sun that came a scant few hours later literally exposed the travesty of it all in broad daylight.

The sliding screens were a twisted mess, the paper completely torn off the smashed-up frames. The tatami-mat floor was scratched and mangled beyond repair. More claw and teeth marks were on the wood supports. The curtains were ripped off the wall and pulverized. It was no longer the Room 201 of Villa Rosa Sasazuka Emi and Chiho knew.

"What...happened here?"

"Maou?! Urushihara?! Camio?! Are you okay?!"

The room's occupants were roughly similar to that of the room itself. The three sat blankly on the floor in a semi-conscious daze. They were surrounding Kinanna, who was loudly snoring in the middle of the room.

"Uh, sorry it's a little untidy in here."

"N-no, um, but what *happened*?"

"He ate it."

"He ate it? Ate what?"

"This lizard freak of nature ate my apartment."

""What?!""

Emi and Chiho couldn't believe it. It looked like a squad of ten cats had spent the past week doing their worst to the room without rest.

"By the time I got back last night, it was already like this. Urushihara and Camio couldn't do a thing about it, but we couldn't kick him outside unattended, and with what happened to the room, we hesitated contacting Amane or the landlord...and the next thing I knew...it was morning."

"W-wait a minute. So that lizard did all this? Uh, he chewed up your closet and the curtains and everything?!"

"Y-y-y-yup..."

"I thought demons didn't need to eat."

"You'd...think so, but..."

"I suppose Kinanna's species demonstrates his anger by chewing and devouring things...*peep*. I have dealt with a large number of demon species, but I have *peep* rarely seen one like this..."

"Thank God he doesn't eat plastic. The dude was trying to eat my computer..."

Upon closer inspection, the sleeves and hems on Urushihara's clothing had bite-sized holes in them. He must have spent the past night gallantly defending his closet territory.

"So he's sleeping now?"

"We caught him. My little trick."

"Trick?"

"Oh, you mean…"

"…Yeah. That."

Chiho guessed it first. She recalled, during Camael's attack on Sasahata North High School, how Urushihara had cast a holy-magic spell that sealed off every door and window in the school complex.

"So he's all better now?"

"*Hell* no. He broke right through the barrier Emilia and Bell made for him. All my trick does is buy us some more time. Before he fell asleep, he ordered us to find something tastier for him to eat. He's just toying with us, dude."

"Oh… I see…"

Emi and Chiho were still standing at the front door, taken aback at the sheer scope of the destruction. Maou was too busy agonizing over the situation to invite them in.

"Now, this isn't gonna kill me or anything, but— How the hell are we gonna explain this to the landlord? We already know she charges for every little thing…" he muttered.

"Wait, hang on, Maou! Didn't you repair the Shuto Expressway when it was falling down? Fixing up a room like this ought to be a snap for you!" Chiho suggested.

She was awfully excited about the idea. Maou, sadly, was not.

"I tried… But he soaks in all the demonic force. And I can't restore anything he's already eaten."

It was true. Kinanna *did* look a measure larger than yesterday.

"And whenever he gets a taste of the dark force, he goes on a rampage all over again. It took us hours just to beat him into submission."

Every escape route was blocked. And for all they knew, when Kinanna woke up again, he'd chew through the floors and walls and start working on Rooms 101 or 202, rendering Nord and Suzuno homeless. But relocating him to one of the other rooms, or somewhere else entirely, would only lead to more mayhem and damage.

"What are we supposed to even feed him...?"

"Well, *you* guys eat regular human food," Emi said. "Why don't you try feeding him whatever lizards eat? I don't really know anything about reptiles, but..."

It sounded like a simple idea. Urushihara promptly shot it down.

"There's no place nearby that sells food for anything besides dogs and cats. We could buy it online, on Jungle or somewhere, but live food takes more time to get delivered, I guess."

""Live food...?""

The two women blanched at the term.

"Yeah. Take a look at this. It's, like, crickets and mealworms, and—"

"Wait, no, Urushihara!"

"Don't show me! That's gross!"

Urushihara was showing them the display from his computer, full of pictures of insects, worms, and other types of reptile food on sale—not the kind of photo album most squeamish people would appreciate seeing.

"What? This isn't that bad, dudettes. It gets worse if you have a large reptile or amphibian, you know. Then they eat, like, cockroach-type things and frozen mice, and..."

"Urushihara!" Chiho protested again.

"I told you to stop! You wanna die?!" Emi threatened.

Urushihara shrugged at their rage and retreated.

"So," Emi continued, "what now...?"

"You know I kept a cat here for a while once, right?" Maou said. "I tried calling Dr. Yoshimura—that was the vet I took him to—and he said it'd be okay to feed him raw chicken, depending on the species. I was thinking we could experiment with that today..."

A while back, Maou took home a kitten who was shivering in the rain, naming it Silverfish. After recuperating for a while in Devil's Castle, the cat was adopted by a man Maou knew who ran a local bicycle shop, referred by the veterinarian Maou had taken the kitten to.

"What if that doesn't work...?"

"I don't want to think about that right now, okay? It's gotta be better for him than sliding doors and tatami mats… I'm sorry. I promise I'll pay you back. The store oughta be open by now—can you go buy us some chicken tenderloin?"

"*Peep…?!*"

That chirp sounded a little fearful to Chiho. She couldn't help but wonder if the term *chicken tenderloin* set off some kind of fight-or-flight reflex in Camio's mind. But unable to bear the sight of this disaster area any longer, they left to carry out Maou's errand for him.

"Good thing Alas Ramus is still asleep," Emi said as they walked, patting her chest.

"Does she have any interest in lizards?"

"She was really fascinated with Camio and Silverfish. She likes any animal she sees. With a lizard like that, she might start reaching for his tail first thing."

Alas Ramus was undoubtedly an animal lover. Her eyes had sparkled the first time she'd met Camio in chicken mode, and during Silverfish's time in Room 201, it had been "I wanna see Meow Meow!" constantly whenever Emi had been home. The ceramic dog Maou had bought for her after the cat was adopted was still on display in Emi's room, a cherished treasure of the child's.

"And lately, whenever there's a documentary about sea life on TV, she's practically glued to the screen. I have to make her sit back so she doesn't mess up her eyes."

"Oh, does she like fish?" asked Chiho.

"We saw this video of a school of spiny lobsters marching across the ocean bottom, and she was completely transfixed." Emi grinned and looked back toward the apartment building. "Either way, angels and demons are one thing, but we really shouldn't be bringing creatures from other planets into the middle of Tokyo. Let's hurry up with this errand."

"Yeah…"

Chiho found herself trying to keep up with Emi's brisk pace. *What's up with her?*

She had the impression Emi was changing a little, again. Exactly how, it was hard to put into words, but it felt even more unusual to Chiho than when she came back from captivity in Ente Isla. The mystery crater in Yoyogi Park, and the "monster" that created it, were now officially a news story. It was the top feature on the MHK TV news broadcast, even. Nobody was hurt, but the impact caused sinkholes to open in several nearby roads, leading to closures. Plus, a giant animal lurking around the virtual dead center of Tokyo led to all kinds of speculation about its origins. Someone illegally importing or keeping a wild animal? Biological terror, maybe? Who knew?

Amane and Suzuno had already worked up a sweat filling the crater in the backyard, but if Kinanna slurped up some more demonic force and kicked up another ruckus, and Maou and his friends couldn't deal with it in time...

"We should buy some thighs, too," Chiho suggested, catching up with Emi. "And some pork. And maybe some sashimi?"

She couldn't have guessed what Kinanna liked, but it had to be better than tatami mats and bare wood. If a larger spread of meat helped them avoid trouble, then all the better.

The reptilian eyes made an almost audible *gleeeeam* as they blinked rapidly.

Perhaps "reptilian" was overstating it. Nobody was sure whether Kinanna the Lenbrellebelve, certified demon, was part of the reptile family at all. But within ten minutes of breaking out their carnivore-oriented spread, Kinanna opened his eyes, immediately setting Maou, Urushihara, and Camio on edge. Ever since he showed up, there was just no telling what this guy might do—and that was especially true for Camio, who had nearly lost his life to him.

"<Mmm... I feel warm.>"

But just as they came to fear Kinanna using his powerful jaw to chomp through the chains of holy energy keeping him down, he took on a much more serene tone of voice.

"<Is the battle over?>"

They hadn't really noticed until yesterday, but Kinanna could speak the standard tongue of the demon realms. Less than standard, actually. His accent was so thick that it was hard even for a native speaker to understand—not because he was trying to speak with a massive gator palate, but because his tone and rhythm were tremendously old-fashioned.

"<Are Legoon's forces not here today?>"

"Legoon? What battle?"

"<I imagine not. With my and Camuinica's powers, not even Legoon could resist us. Satan, bring me Camuinica. I need to see his magical sword.>"

"Um, umm, wait a minute—oh, I mean <Wait a minute. What are you talking about?>"

"<The sword. The magical sword! Bring me Nothung.>"

"<Nothung?>" Maou repeated.

It was one of the Devil Overlord's relics, already discovered by Camio and installed inside the Devil's Castle on Ente Isla.

"<Nothung. Do I need to spell it out for you? Nothung! Camuinica would have it, Satan, and my job is to sharpen it. Nothung... Nothung...>"

"...What do you think?" Maou asked Urushihara and Camio, going back to Japanese.

"I have no idea." The former shrugged. "You think he's lost his marbles or something?"

"I wonder the same *cheep* thing," Camio added, debuting a brand-new bird noise along the way. "Ever since I encountered the angel Camael at the cave where this *cheep*ture...er, creature lives, Kinanna has been convinced I am *cheep* Camuinica."

"Try to keep the high-pitched cheeping down, Camio. But maybe you're both right."

Mistaking people for others. Eating unusual things. Making nonsensical statements. Among humans, these were the classic symptoms of dementia.

"If I could venture a *cheep* guess, this Kinanna may very well be the oldest demon in our realms. Among those of my clan, the Pájaro Danino, Camuinica is not a very common name. And if this Kinanna knew my ancestors personally, then I wonder if the Satan he speaks of..."

"It's probably *the* Devil Overlord Satan, isn't it?" Maou gulped nervously as Urushihara gave Kinanna a closer look.

"Based on what the *cheep* angel outcast and his band tell me, the Devil Overlord's relics are actually the subject of a great deal of folklore and traditions. In the case of the Nothung, legends of it being wielded by Camuinica have been passed down over generations...although not, I am saddened to say, by the *cheep* Pájaro themselves."

The Spear of Adramelechinus was, of course, passed down through Adramelech and his clan—and in similar fashion, the Nothung was a treasure of the Pájaro Danino. The fact that Camio, current head of the Pájaro, wasn't aware of this no doubt embarrassed him.

"I guess," Maou reflected, "a lot of this stuff was closer at hand than we thought."

It certainly helped that, as Lord of All Demons, he was able to tap into a wealth of information and leads others couldn't. The Sorcery of the False Gold, an ancient tome and another relic, was tracked down following interviews with a litany of demons. It turned out to be the property of a now-vanquished demon clan, hidden within what used to be their lands. Camio sent vast groups of soldiers to comb the lands, and they finally found the Sorcery in what was once a smelting furnace.

"However, there are more than a few tales that speak of the Astral Gem as the 'collar' of the Lenbrellebelve, and only Kinanna matches the descriptions given in the legends that survived..."

"Yeah, and if Kinanna personally knew Satanael and Camuinica, it's gotta be him beyond a reasonable doubt, right?"

There was still concern on Maou's face, but an excited smile was rapidly replacing his hesitation.

"That *is* lucky. Now, not only do we have a relic, but we have someone who might tell us what happened between heaven and the demon realms. Or what Satanael got up to."

"You think?" Urushihara gave him an indifferent look, the thought of learning more about a father he only barely remembered not seeming to move him much. "Because, dude, it's pretty clear from the past twenty-four hours that his brain's scrambled. You think we're gonna get what we want from him? I mean, we're talking millennia's worth of memories."

"<The Nothung… The Nothung…>"

"Well, thanks to Camio being here, I think that might dredge up some memories related to his dad. I hope anyway. He already brought up Satanael and Camuinica…and Legoon, which I'm still not sure what that is."

Neither Maou nor Urushihara had heard the term before. But given that Camio ran into Camael while making contact with Kinanna, it was easy to imagine that it referred to someone in heaven.

"<Yes… Legoon; we must fend off Legoon. Quickly… Camuinica, what are you doing? You're late, Camuinica… The blade of the Nothung will be so dull and fractured!>"

"Okay. One, let's feed him. Two, let's ask Laila and Gabriel if the term *Legoon* rings any bells."

"But if Legoon is an angel, how come this lizard didn't react to me—or Laila or Emilia?" Urushihara asked. "We *are* kind of angel adjacent, my friends."

"Well, of course…" Maou was about to brush the idea off—until he realized he couldn't. "Ahh, actually, I don't know about that. Maybe it's because you guys don't look the part?"

"Look the part?"

"Yeah. I mean, you and Laila both have purple hair. When Miki Shiba was here, you spent the whole time in the closet, so he didn't see you. Maybe the combo of silver hair and red eyes is the key?"

"Maybe, but then Sariel and Raguel won't set him off, either. Then again, this is a half-brain-dead lizard. Who knows if there's even a one-to-one connection in his mind?"

"Well, if he's fine now, let's just forget about it. We can't expect to solve all our problems immediately. After that..." Maou examined his surroundings. "I'm gonna have to tell Ashiya about this room. *And* my rejection."

"You really think that's important right now...?"

"Considering what's coming up, yeah. In several ways."

"I have to wonder about that..."

"Hey, we're back... Oh, he's awake! I'll whip something up right now, okay?"

At that moment, Chiho and Emi, respectively, arrived back from shopping, bags in hand.

"We wound up buying a bunch of stuff. You guys haven't had anything to eat today, have you?"

The smells made Maou and Urushihara suddenly remember their empty stomachs. It also made Kinanna stop repeating the word *Nothung* long enough to lift his nose into the air, sniffing at it.

"Fried chicken is such a powerful thing..."

Maou slumped back in his seat, relaxed. Urushihara, Emi, and Chiho nodded their agreement.

It turned out Kinanna had little interest in raw meat but was all over the deep-fried chicken pieces Chiho brought for her friends. He gobbled up three whole packs of them—how he had room for them in his stomach was a mystery—and now fully satisfied, he was snoring yet again. It shocked everyone. Virtually anyone not on a vegetarian diet enjoyed fried chicken, but apparently that flavor profile worked just fine with the palates of ancient reptilian demons from another world, as well.

"I have very *peep* conflicted feelings about this."

Only Camio, who was nearly made into chicken curry once, was distressed by it. But a peaceful Kinanna was a blissful thing to see, even if it meant no chicken for the humans in the room. To deal with that, Chiho walked into the apartment, paying careful mind to the frayed tatami mats underfoot, and made some egg-infused pork and rice. The results finally helped Maou and Urushihara kick back a little.

"Mommy, what's that?"

"Hmm, what indeed? Daddy and I aren't sure, either."

Now Alas Ramus was awake, keeping her distance atop Emi's lap as she looked at Kinanna. Emi kept her there mainly to prevent the child from getting splinters running on the floor.

"Bowwow?"

"No, not a bowwow. This is a, um, lizard, I guess?"

"Lizzerd? Meow meow?"

"No, not at *all* a meow meow."

Alas Ramus's reptile-related vocabulary wasn't too developed yet, so she tried applying every other animal name she knew instead.

"But what is he to *us*? I understand that he might know about the fight between Satanael and Ignora, but aren't we more concerned about the Astral Gem right now?"

"We're still not sure he's related to the Gem," Maou retorted. "And he might know about other relics, too. He knows stuff that we don't, and it might give us some hints for our battle, you know?"

"But we're talking about things that happened thousands of years ago. Can we really apply any of that?"

As Emi pointed out, even if Kinanna was around to see any fighting, it would have been when the angels were still busy colonizing Ente Isla's moon, an era before human life existed on that planet entirely. They didn't know if they could extract that kind of history from him, but it might not matter to their current plan anyway.

"Actually, I'm thinking that we can," Maou confidently replied. "Remember what Gabriel said? Only a very small percentage of people actually 'work' up in heaven. And maybe that applies to more than just its military. If nobody's really working to advance society, that means its tech is gonna lag behind, too, right?"

"Maybe, but it's not gonna stay frozen for thousands of years."

"Of course not. But I don't think it'd hurt us if we studied some of the basics about how they work. For example, they weren't just camping out in tents, right? If we can get an idea of their settlements, or their towns, or what kind of equipment and weapons they have, that'll let us react faster if something comes up."

"Could we ask Gabriel or Sariel about that?" Chiho asked. "I think they'd know a lot about what heaven's like these days... Laila, too."

Maou and Urushihara exchanged glances.

"Chiho Sasaki," the latter stated deadpan, "do you really think we can rely on them as impartial sources?"

"Huh?"

That seemed to surprise the girl. But the others were serious.

"In the case of Laila, at least," Maou added, "we've already gotten everything useful out of her that we can. And from that, I can tell that she doesn't know much about fighting."

He recalled Laila attempting to fend off a berserk Erone. It didn't end well for her. She clearly had nothing.

"She's not totally useless in a fight, but that's just talking about her as an individual. I guess her original job was a doctor, so it's not like she'll have a broad insight into heaven's military strength. And even if she did, she's been out of heaven for at least a few centuries. She's an unreliable source."

"And Gabriel and Sariel would be worse," added Emi, looking even more dubious than Maou. "This fight isn't some kind of video game where you beat the last boss, then the ending plays for you. We're gonna have to live in the world that's there after it's over. In the society that already exists in it."

A quick-and-dirty list of the forces gathered to face off against Ignora, the god that rules Ente Isla's heavens, would include:

Maou, Ashiya, Urushihara, Camio, the Malebranche chieftains, and the rest of the demon realm's denizens.

Saint Aile's elite knight corps and the Holy Magic Administrative Institute, led by Rumack and Emeralda respectively.

The Reconciliation Panel, led by Suzuno, and the subset of Church clerics involved with it.

Efzahan's eight imperial knight corps, in the service of Ashiya on behalf of the Azure emperor.

A select few people from the alien nation of Japan, including Chiho, Emi's friend Rika Suzuki, and Amane Ohguro.

The children of Ente Isla's Sephirah, including Alas Ramus, Acieth, and Erone.

Gabriel and Laila, more or less defectors from heaven.

Emi and Nord, citizens of Saint Aile.

They had all gathered under the same flag with the same goals, but this was a motley crew from an extremely diverse set of backgrounds. Among them, only Albert and Urushihara could reliably be credited with being involved just to save the human race. Albert was born on the Northern Island but had traveled the world as the Hero's friend in support of Emi and Emeralda. He had no particular attachment to his homeland, and he was happy being anywhere at any time. And while Urushihara was living with Maou at the moment, that was strictly because of the advantages it offered to his future; he did not feel any particular responsibility for how the world would turn out afterward.

The rest, however, didn't share that opinion. They all had roots firmly implanted somewhere, and after the dust settled, they had to make sure the buds that sprouted stayed protected. Maou and Ashiya had an obligation to carve out a future for the demon realms and its residents. Rumack and the Azure Emperor had their own nations to serve, and Emi and Nord had the Western Island village of Sloane, a homeland awaiting their return.

To Gabriel and Sariel, the heavens were really the only place they could call home. They might have forsaken it long ago, yes, but the goal of this mission wasn't to kill every angel in heaven. It was to stop Ignora from pulling the strings of Ente Isla's history and rescue Alas Ramus's brothers and sisters. And as long as it was, someone would have to think about what to do with the angels in a post-Ignora landscape. Perhaps Gabriel and Sariel would return to their angelic comrades—and as a result, perhaps they were hiding some pertinent information from their current allies, even if it damaged the force's overall chances.

"Of course, I think this all might be the last thing on Sariel's mind right now, but…"

""Ah...""

Chiho and Emi grinned, fully convinced of that. But Maou was serious.

"It's not funny. There's no telling if Ms. Kisaki's transfer might trigger a change of heart for him. Maybe he'll decide he can't bear a world where she never gives him the time of day, rejoins his old friends, and fights against us. There's a non-zero chance of that, if you ask me. And even if he doesn't go that far, he might try to get in our way here in Japan."

If that happens, the Sephirah of Earth—Amane and Shiba, to name two—wouldn't take that sitting down. But it still meant Sariel would be a thorn in their side.

"Maybe I should have killed him back then, after all?"

Emi recalled all the insulting things Sariel had said to her when he'd first come to Japan. That and the murderous rage they summoned within her.

"Y'know, I think the same thing whenever he causes trouble for Kisaki, but can you stop with the murder talk in front of Alas Ramus?"

"..."

Emi, who had blurted out the word *kill* with barely a second thought, brought a hand to her mouth.

"Whuhh?"

Alas Ramus curiously looked up at this, her smile indicating she didn't think anything of Mommy's thirst for blood.

"It's too late for that anyway," Maou said. "Besides, if you think that Gabriel and Sariel are fully on our side, I think you're sorta wrong about that."

"What do you mean?"

"I-it's not like one thing or the other happened, but between what Gabriel told us, and what I knew before, and what I thought of on the way to Chi's zirga... I can't really put my finger on it yet, but something's weird."

"Weird?"

"I don't remember everything—like, I ignored a lot of it, because I didn't think *this* would happen until fairly recently—but you know, it just doesn't add up. Every little incident, I mean. Or rather, that each individual incident doesn't make sense together, but then *they* show up, and suddenly it's all linked together."

He was being unusually vague. As he'd warned Emi, his thoughts were still disorganized about this.

"Yeah. You might be right. I'd like to think I have a good handle on things based on what Mother told me, but there are still a lot of answers we don't have. I'm not sure any of them will have a direct impact on this battle, but I kind of get why you have a bad feeling about it."

Watching Emi nod at him, face taut with concern, Chiho noticed something else entirely. Now she could see what about Emi had struck her as odd: It wasn't a drastic change, but it *was* a change—now, whenever she talked to Maou, Emi was meekly accepting the things he said. Normally, if Maou was being this vague, she'd be sure to jab at him a little before giving her own opinions.

"But how long are you gonna try to talk to that lizard? Do you really have the time to waste on him?"

Or maybe she hadn't changed at all, actually. Chiho found herself rapidly reconsidering her observation. It was just hard to figure out Emi lately.

"Practically speaking," Maou replied, "we still don't know if we've found the Astral Gem. Until we know for sure, I don't see why chatting with Grandpa a little is a problem."

"Are you sure the lizard is a grandpa, by the way? Not a grandma?" Urushihara interjected bluntly.

"Whatever," Maou replied with a shrug. "And also, we're kind of free until the Devil's Castle in Ente Isla is all fixed up. Either way, we got pretty much nothing else to do. Camio's hurt bad, and we have no idea where Camael is, so we can't go searching in the demon realms quite yet. So why don't we focus on keeping this lizard fed and happy for a little while?"

"Raising an elderly lizard to save the world, huh...? I was kind of hoping we could go beat up someone, and he'd give us a hint or something." Emi sighed.

"That *would* be more up your alley, wouldn't it?"

"Yeah, and that's why this whole thing's annoying me. But oh, well. Lucifer and Bell and Alciel can't come back here all that often anyway, and we all know how Camio is."

And then Emi said something that shocked Chiho, Urushihara, and Maou all at once:

"I can stop by to lizard-sit from time to time."

""""Huh?!"""""

"But if we're both at work, you're gonna have to figure something out." Emi looked Maou straight in the eye. "And all I'm gonna do is watch him. If he starts rambling about the good ol' days of the demon realms, I never said I'd listen. And also, if this is how it's gonna be for a while, you're gonna have to fess up to the landlord about this place and have her fix it up. If I'm here, that means Alas Ramus will be, too, remember. If she cuts her hands or feet or gets something in her eyes, that's gonna be trouble, all right?"

"""..."""

"Y-yeah..."

Urushihara and Chiho were speechless. Maou wasn't far behind.

"And you'd like that, too, huh, Alas Ramus? Now you'll be at Daddy's home more than ever!"

"Rilly?!"

And while the three of them were too shocked to reply, Emi started egging Alas Ramus about it. That sealed the deal.

Certainly, Emi volunteering to watch Kinanna was exactly what Maou wanted. But this was so perplexing. Emi nominated herself for the job before anyone could say anything else. Maou didn't consider her part of the Kinanna team anyway, and Emi virtually never paid any respect to his needs.

He couldn't help but double-check.

"But um, are you sure?"

"Is there a problem?"

His question was met with another question.

"No. No problem. I appreciate it. Thanks."

Now the Hero had the Devil King's permission to enter and leave Devil's Castle whenever she wanted. And while this was no longer the bombshell it would have been at one point, any visit up to now was more forced on Emi's part and only grudgingly accepted on Maou's.

Thus was birthed a historical moment. But…

"Are you sure you want to go that far, Yusa? I mean, helping Maou out like that?"

Chiho found herself asking that as they walked back from Villa Rosa Sasazuka.

For a while now, Chiho liked to imagine a future where Maou and Emi could coexist as neighbors. Emi had certainly relaxed her stance as of late. She and Maou were seeing each other so much now that Chiho envied them a little.

But this felt like something different. It was hard to be sure, since Emi was getting looser with him in general, but before now, that meant three things: She'd do her best not to bring her personal beefs with her to work; she stopped griping about everything Maou did; and she wouldn't hesitate to work with him if they shared a common goal. Camio talked how about they were still enemies, but today, she used her own time and money for Maou's sake. She poked her nose into his affairs. She even promised her assistance in the future. Chiho wasn't childish enough to add it all together and think Yusa was harboring feelings for Maou, but she still wanted to clear the doubt from her mind.

But Emi openly nodded at the question.

"Maybe…I shouldn't have, no. Was it that easy to spot?"

She sounded a bit anxious. Previously, whenever she did something to help Maou in the end, she'd always bite back or obfuscate the subject if someone pointed it out to her. "I don't think Maou noticed, no…"

"Maybe Lucifer did. He's weirdly observant about that kind of thing."

Emi frowned. Frowned, despite smiling just a moment ago over making Maou owe her a favor.

"Mommy, you okeh?"

Alas Ramus's eyebrows arched upward in worry as Emi pulled her along. "Yeah, I'm fine. I'm fine...but a little anxious."

"Not anxious about Grandpa Kinanna, I assume."

Something about Chiho adding that honorific to the name of a lizard seemed so unbeatably *like* her. It gave Emi the smile she was hoping to find. "I wish everybody stayed the same as much as you do."

"Huh?"

"...I'm sorry, can we rest for a moment?"

The park they were passing by was a common site for Ashiya and Suzuno to take Alas Ramus out to, back before she fused with Emi's holy sword.

"Are you okay?"

Chiho, sitting next to the downtrodden Emi on a bench, peered at her face through her long hair.

"Listen, Chiho. Do you think the Devil King is still a *king*, really?"

"Hmm?"

"When this battle is over, what do you think he's gonna do?"

"...You mean if you beat Ignora and release Alas Ramus's brothers and sisters?"

"It's gonna set the gears of history in motion for Ente Isla, whether we want it to or not. What's gonna happen to him and his realm then?"

"You'll lose holy magic."

After returning from the chaos on the Eastern Island, Miki Shiba—landlord of Villa Rosa Sasazuka and eleventh personification of Earth's Sephirah—broke the news in Urushihara's hospital room: If the people of Ente Isla kept using holy or demonic force at the current rate, they'd be annihilated before long. Holy energy was spiritual energy, something flowing all around the planet. If it dissipated over time, the souls needed to fill a body would go unborn, and the human population would dissipate with it. Normally, the children of the Sephirah would support the growth of human civilization, preventing so many people from harvesting the vast wells of energy holy and demonic force could produce. That wasn't happening here.

"Not 'lose,' so much as we won't be able to use it, is how I think it'll work. But really, nobody knows what'll happen once we release Alas Ramus's siblings."

For a sorcerer, it was the same thing.

"But that energy was a given to the whole world. Gradually losing the ability to harness it is probably gonna trigger a panic. People will search for new energy sources, and I'm sure it'll lead to wars. Anything that relies on holy energy or sorcery will need to change."

"But that's what General Rumack and Wurs and everyone on the Eastern Island is there to help with, right?"

"Well, who knows how it'll actually work out? Whether it's General Rumack, Lady Wurs, or the Azure Emperor, they're all gonna have to focus on their own nation first. That's a given. There's never gonna be a future where nobody dies. We'll save the human race from total annihilation, but there's still going to be fighting. By that point, though, I'll no longer be the Hero."

She may have been half-angel, but much of Emi's power depended on holy energy. Without it, the Hero Emilia—or really, the human Emilia Justina…

"I'll just be a person. And depending on how fast the world changes, I might not be much different from anyone else in Japan. Slash at me with a sword, and you might just kill me. No more flying. If I jump off somewhere high, I'll probably break my legs. If I break my legs, I'll need months to recover from it. And if that's what happens…"

Emi sighed, her voice quiet and shaky. She looked upward.

"He'll still be king. Ruling over his people. The demons."

There were many more humans participating in the assault on heaven than demons. Emi was strictly talking about holy energy, but if Shiba was to be believed, the release of the Sephirah would bring a sea of changes to demonic energy as well. What would happen to the demons then? They'd struggle to survive, of course. But without demonic force, where were they going to find energy to live off of? The answer was obvious. Emi had predicted it long ago. She'd seen how much Maou, Ashiya, and Urushihara enjoyed the food they had at home.

They might decide to invade Ente Isla again, before their demon energy fully vanished, in search of "something" to replace it. Who would be their leader? Who would fend them off? If this invasion took place before the demonic force disappeared, then holy energy would still be around as well.

"Is there anything that's really tethering him to Japan at the moment? Something that'll keep him from doing something…stupid again, before this battle is over?"

Emi was expecting more. She had hoped Maou would be accepted as a full-time employee in this world. That he'd then live out his life in Japan. That, even if drastic measures were needed for it, he'd keep staying in this world as Sadao Maou for as long as possible. She had known long ago that Maou was serious about becoming a part of life in Japan. Now, though, one pathway to that goal was cut off from him. The path to full-time employment, the tether keeping him on Earth, was closed. And in a very short time, he'd be faced with a choice leading him down some other path. A choice where Satan's personal desires—a life among humans, a full-time job—would no longer get to be a priority.

He was still beloved and followed by many as the Lord of All Demons. Emi knew that loyalty and respect hadn't changed, even when their king was forced into the body of a human. He couldn't possibly abandon all those supporters. And if he couldn't, he would have to fight.

But with whom?

Chiho watched as Alas Ramus picked up a branch at her feet and used it to draw mysterious abstract art in the ground.

"I don't like this. I've been saying since forever that I didn't want you and Maou to fight, but…"

"…Yeah."

"Whether it's Suzuno or Emeralda or Albert, or Wurs or Rumack, or Ashiya or Urushihara, or Camio or Farlo or Libicocco or Ciri-atto… I don't want anyone to fight anybody."

For now, they were able to be together in the same place. To make chocolate treats together. Why, at the moment they remove something twisting the world away from what it needs to be, does all of that have to fall apart? Because that's the world. That's nations; that's politics; that's economics; that's people. She didn't need anyone to tell her that.

To everyone fighting against heaven here, this battle was just a destination. And once they got back from it, they'd have to live in the place they chose. But what if, over there, survival became a question? They'd have to fight to live.

Emi's groaning seemed to take physical form in the air, plopping to the ground like mud.

"After fighting for so long, the seeds for the next battle between human and demon are already growing. How long do I have to go before I get some rest?"

"Yeah… I know."

"I don't care who it is. I just want someone to make his dreams come true. Then I wouldn't have to stay up worrying about whether I'm going to make this child have a sad experience."

The chief mission of the battle against heaven was to release Alas Ramus's siblings. But what would a grown Alas Ramus do if she found out being released meant her beloved mommy and daddy would have to fight each other? Would she love the world, the way she did now? Would they wind up like Caiel and Sikeena, who tried to destroy Ignora and Satanael's research?

A *full-time employee*. It sounded like such a stupid term, given the context. Economic downturn or not, vast numbers of people became full-time employees in Japan—every year, every month, every day. Why couldn't such a studious, serious-minded, talented person like him join them? These days, it wasn't uncommon for a new college grad to get rejected from dozens of firms before finding something. Just because Maou got rejected by one, it'd be far too hasty to assume the dream was done forever. But apart from his own desires, Maou had no particular reason to be a full-timer. He'd have a perfectly normal life either way. He didn't have to save up money for marriage or children; he didn't have elderly parents to take care of; and he didn't have to worry about his retirement budget. He made it this far simply out of his desire to do so.

"Plus, I've told him how much I love him, and he still hasn't given me an answer..."

Chiho deliberately kept her tone light, like the observation didn't matter to her.

"If you can't stop him, Chiho, I'm not sure anyone can."

Stewing over a question without an answer gets you nowhere but feeling down. Chiho tried to end the topic there, but Emi knew how she felt about it. She smiled at her as she stood up.

"Chiho?"

"Yeah?"

"I..."

"...Yeah?"

"Seeing him try his best in Japan... I guess I don't hate that."

Chiho beamed. "...I can tell."

She turned to Emi, smiling happily, while her friend's smile was chagrined.

"It'd be nice if this works out," Chiho pressed.

"I have no idea what that would look like, to be hon—"

"Chi! Saemi!"

Suddenly, they heard a voice behind them. They turned around, surprised; Alas Ramus stood up to see what was going on...and there, on the road outside the park, they found a woman in a business suit waving at them.

"Ms. Kisaki!"

"...You smell like Magrobad!"

✳

"Are you serious...?"

"Would I joke about this to you?"

Ashiya was seated on the small tatami-mat floor section of Devil's Castle on Ente Isla, his long legs folded in front of him. He was watching Laila, who had just stood up in surprise, eyes wide open.

"I thought about going by myself," he continued, "but you volunteered first the other day. A second or third time would not be any different."

'Of—of course it wouldn't! He's never going to listen to me…'

"I will make him," he coldly replied. "We have no time. The link between Kinanna and the Astral Gem is still unclear, but there is still every chance we will have all four relics by this time tomorrow. Once we do, that triggers the final battle. And you know full well that we need all our eggs in one basket beforehand."

"But…"

"As I'm sure you know, you cannot tell anyone about this. Especially not Emilia—or Emeralda Etuva. And not Crestia Bell or Hazel Rumack, either."

"Wh-what about Albert?" she asked.

"…He will be the first to learn of it either way," Ashiya said after a moment of deliberation. "But now is not the time."

"B-but what if it gets discovered before battle begins? Won't defeating Ignora be the last of our worries then? It'll take all of us gathered here and tear us apart."

"That will not happen if you keep your mouth shut."

"!"

The force of Ashiya's demonic presence made Laila gasp.

"The truth is, it has not been discovered yet. However, the Azure Emperor and a subset of the Efzahan generals are aware of my plan," Ashiya continued ruthlessly.

Despite that, it was clear who had the upper hand in these negotiations.

"We are not the only ones running out of time," he insisted. "If I had to guess… His Demonic Highness's application for a permanent position was turned down."

"What?!"

Maou had never said so himself, but Ashiya was all but sure of it.

"When my liege entered training, he was convinced he would be accepted. The other day, however, I detected none of that conviction, none of that aspiration. If he *was* accepted, he would have sprinted over to tell me first. And with that great hope of his going unrealized, if we let any more time pass without making a move, His Demonic Highness may be thrust into a brand-new wilderness."

This statement was, to be frank, a mere threat on Ashiya's part. Even if Maou recovered his full majesty as Satan, the Devil King, he would doubtlessly avoid taking the path Laila imagined, the one Ashiya threatened her with. But being honest about that would be a terrible negotiating tactic.

"It is time to decide, Angel, because we of the demons have already chosen our path for the future."

He paused, waiting for just the right timing to drive in the final blow.

"I want you to link me to Chief Herder Dhin Dhem Wurs."

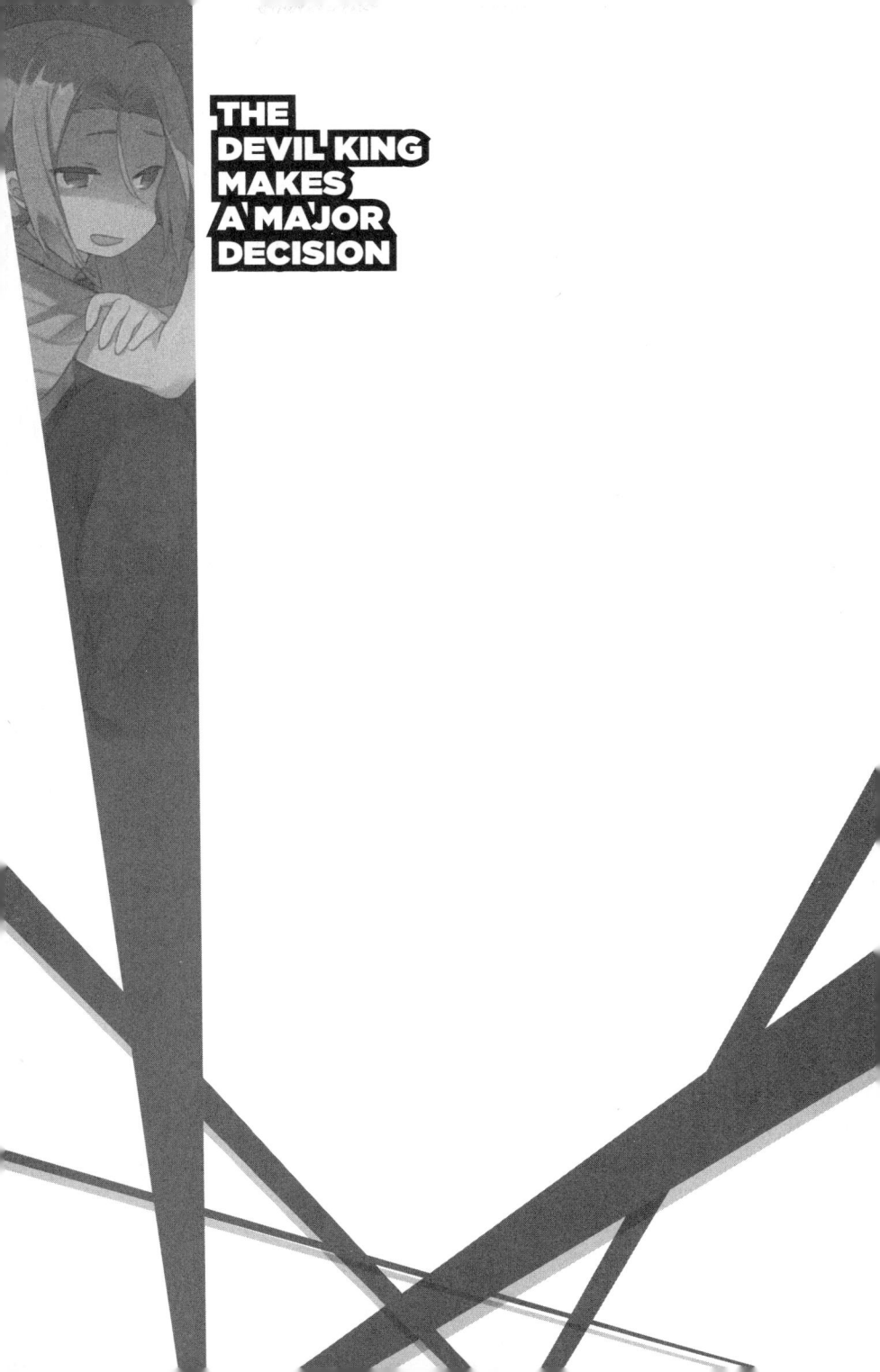

THE DEVIL KING MAKES A MAJOR DECISION

"Hahhhh..."

"..."

It was afternoon, past the lunch rush, and Maou's sighs echoed across the dining space.

"Ahhh..."

Then, with the evening shift, a forlorn groan emanated from the staff break room.

"..."

"It's audible from here again..."

"Yeah..."

The crew behind Emi was chatting about it.

"Ughhh... Gahh..."

The sighs and wails as he performed the post-dinner back-end check were impossible to ignore.

"Hey!"

"...Huh?"

It was ten at night, and Emi's shift was over. Changing out of her uniform, she patted Maou's shoulder in the back room, then brought her hand to her hip.

"Can you stop moaning and groaning like that? You're messing up *my* motivation, too."

"Ahh…"

Maou just hung his head, the life gone from his face.

"I'm sorry. I'm just kind of tired…ugh…"

Another sigh, right in front of her.

"You're not keeping healthy habits, are you? You acted like you bounced back from it, but you've been terrible ever since you got rejected."

"Ah, shut up. I haven't been able to sleep lately…"

An irritated Maou attempted to defend himself. The attempt quickly petered out, lost in the halls of his darkened face. "You try living like this. Every single damn evening, that brain-dead lizard wakes me up. I'm so worried he's up to something, I can't focus on anything."

He was referring to Kinanna, of course.

"Because if he does do something, I'm the only one who can deal with it. Ashiya's not in Devil's Castle; he said he had some kind of extended business in Ente Isla. Camio's still a *chicken*, Urushihara and Suzuno can't be there every day, and I really can't beg Amane or the landlord for help unless things really go south. And the idea of leaving him to Acieth hasn't even occurred to me."

"But Bell's commuting back there daily, isn't she? You ought to trust her a little more."

"It's not a matter of trust. Whenever I get back home, I still gotta take responsibility for everything. It's not like having someone else there makes me feel any better."

"…It's really that bad?"

"Not as bad as when he was gnawing on the closet, but…" Maou, squinting like he was dealing with a headache, began counting off an imaginary checklist with his fingers. "He starts screaming in the middle of the night; he gets his tongue all over everything; he takes a crap on my futon…"

"Uh…"

Emi winced. This was not the kind of conversation two on-duty restaurant employees should have been having…but it at least gave her some insight into why he was so deeply exhausted.

"We've spoiled him food-wise, so he doesn't want the fried chicken anymore. He whines about how hungry he is ten minutes after he eats. If we don't feed him, he gets violent. He mistakes Camio for Camuinica and comes *this* close to lunging at him..."

"Wait. Isn't he restrained? You didn't tell me about any of this. I'm supposed to watch him most of the day tomorrow for the first time."

Emi had volunteered to watch Kinanna at Devil's Castle a while back, but her shifts for the next week were already set in stone at the time. It would be the first day she'd be alone in Devil's Castle with him.

"He's a living thing. I can't just shackle him to the wall; what if I kill him? We still don't know how the Astral Gem connects to that guy."

When they had first captured him, that was essentially what they had done—Maou asking Emi and Suzuno to magically bind him down with holy energy. Nowadays, he had his own cardboard box alongside Camio's, covered in a clear holy-magic case.

"The thing is," Maou explained with a sigh, "when he starts getting all wild, he knocks the box over. If I try keeping it upright, it breaks. I can't, like, bolt it to the floor or anything."

"Huh?"

If they were capable of tapping into mystical powers to form a magical cube around this space-alien demonic lizard, finding a hammer and a few nails didn't seem to be much more effort to Emi.

"S-Suzuno told me," stammered Maou, seeing Emi's disbelief on her face. "Even now, Kinanna's still in an incredibly weakened state. If we expose him to really strong sorcery or holy force for an extended period of time, she's worried that might shorten his life."

"What, that it'd purify him to death?"

"If we screw it up, yeah. I dunno how many millennia he's been alive, but the way she put it, she'd never forgive us if we mess something up with him, he atrophies to death, and we lose everything..."

"All right, but if he's knocking around the box you're holding... I mean *keeping* him in, what if he hurts himself?"

"I know, all right? But I don't see any perfect solution. I tried asking Suzuno for a stronger metal cage or something lighter I could hang from a pole or something, but if he wants out of it, he always finds a way. Imagine you're sleeping, and all of a sudden the corner of a metal cage hits you on the head. It's not even funny how much that hurts. Luckily, it happened to me and not Camio, or else he'd just be dead. And his mind's so out of whack, every time he acts up, it's with his full strength. I just can't deal with him…"

In other words, Maou was at his wit's end because of a grandpa stressing him out. That might be something he could overlook a little if this were a blood relative or someone he owed a great debt to but to Maou, Kinanna was even less than a total stranger. The only reason they kept him was because, out of all the legends and traditions Camio had collected about the Astral Gem, he was the closest match in description. But if Camio described the Lenbrellebelve as a clan, there had to be at least a few of them around. For all they knew, maybe they all had the stonelike growth Kinanna did. They were betting otherwise, but for the time being, they weren't even entirely sure what they were betting on. Maou was counting on gleaning some info on ancient times from him, but if all he had told Emi about was the pain of dealing with him, she doubted he had found out much over the last week-ish.

"So… I'm sorry. I'll try not to get in anyone's away, but just go easy on me today. I'm really tired…"

Emi didn't think he was exaggerating. Taking care of an elderly patient put huge mental, physical, and economic stresses on the caregiver. But at least you didn't have to worry about that patient absorbing demonic force and carving huge craters in the ground. The exact measure of Kinanna's strength was an unknown, but he had already gravely injured Camio—and if he didn't have full control of his mental faculties, there was no guessing what sort of trouble he might cause next.

In the worst case, Emi thought, they might just have to consider taking his life. But based on what Maou had told her, she wasn't so sure where the worst case lay with him any longer.

"All right. Sorry I was mean to you."

"...Huh?"

"I'll stay in Bell's apartment tonight. You're closing tonight, too, right? I'll take care of anything that happens, so just try to stay focused for the next two hours or so, okay?"

"Yeah...but what's up with you?"

"What?"

Through his fatigue, Maou blinked, his face tightening. "You're just being so weirdly kind to me."

"I'm covering for you because you're being a pain to everyone else at work. Don't get the wrong idea."

"...My bad."

"It's not the first time. What's up with *you*?"

"Uhh..."

"Well, see you."

"Thanks..."

Emi wrapped up the conversation before he could form a response.

The cold no longer chilled to the bone these days. Normally, as part of her commute, she'd board a train at Hatagaya Station for Meidaimae, but this time, she opted to walk to Villa Rosa Sasazuka. Given what Maou had said, she wanted to hurry right there.

✳

"I didn't expect to see *you* two at this park... Oh, who's that?"

The previous day, when Kisaki ran into Emi and Chiho at the park, the first thing she noticed was Alas Ramus at their feet. It made her smile.

"If she's with you right now, were you just at Marko's place?"

"Hiiii!" Alas Ramus waved excitedly once their eyes met.

"Well, hello there," Kisaki replied with a smile. "But I don't see Daddy around...?"

"Um... We're watching him at the moment," Chiho said. "He's got a few things to deal with right now."

From a standpoint of regular common sense, Kisaki didn't have a high opinion of Maou asking Chiho for help caring for Alas Ramus.

As far as she knew, the child was Maou's relative, and if she was here, it meant she must have been staying at Maou's place. If she went and called Emi Mommy right now, Chiho knew it would turn things pretty chaotic with Kisaki.

Emi, perhaps realizing this, stiffened a bit. But Kisaki just nodded at Chiho.

"Yeah, Marko's got a lot on his plate, huh? Is it all right if I ask what's up?"

A crazed magical lizard had eaten half of his apartment. It actually sounded like a safe enough thing to say to her, but she'd never believe it. Thus, Chiho opted for a "mostly truthful" approach.

"Well… Maou's, um, grandfather got hurt pretty bad, so he's taking care of him."

"Oh…" Kisaki frowned. "Well, I know he's too proud to accept charity from me, but could you guys do me a favor? If you could kinda hint to him for me that, you know, if it gets really bad, I can be flexible with the shift schedule? I've been in that position myself, and I know how it can drive you insane sometimes. And not that it's for me to say, but try to give him a hand if you can, okay? Don't go crazy, but…"

"All right. I'll tell him that."

"Thanks. Because I'm sure he has enough on his plate as it is."

Emi and Chiho knew exactly what Kisaki was talking about.

"Yeah," Emi said, before deciding to venture a question. "Um, if he didn't get accepted then, was that his only chance, or…?"

"No, not at all."

""Oh?!"" they both exclaimed at once.

"But it's gonna be a year before he can try again. At the earliest."

"Ohh, I see."

In other words, they only offered managerial testing once a year.

"At the earliest, though?"

"I forget if I told you or not, but floor crewmembers need a recommendation from their manager to undertake the training. This time around, he needed approval from me, as his manager, and then the area manager above me…although, with the area manager, it's pretty much a sign-and-forget thing."

"Oh, but..."

It dawned on Emi.

"But it's not necessarily a given that the next manager will do that, right? She may not even want to give him a nod, in the worst case. Which, you know, I've met with your new manager several times, but we haven't made the official handover yet. I'm not sure if she's willing to accept my suggestions for recommendations or not."

A manager of a MgRonald was just that—a manager, bearing full responsibility for everything related to that location. For all they knew, the new manager might want to shake things up and go against the previous one's strategies.

"Also, frankly, Marko's just too useful where he is. He's serious about work, he's precise, he's trained in a lot of positions, and he's super-flexible with his hours. If we recommend him for management, and he gets accepted, we'd need to find someone to replace him, and at his level, that's tough. If the new manager doesn't think finding a proper replacement is possible, she may decide to use Maou's previous rejection as a reason not to recommend him again to keep him where he is. We see that a lot..."

As Kisaki put it, whenever a new manager was assigned to a location that put up good sales results the previous fiscal year, that resulted in a hefty amount of pressure. Good sales meant a talented manager at the helm, leading a good, well-trained crew. A new manager entering such a location faced two obstacles—one, how to keep the wave going, and two, how to get the crew to accept their leadership. If a location manned by people like multiyear veterans and housewives working part-time notched good results, they could revolt against a new manager who didn't follow the old one's lead. They'd judge every move they made, spreading all sorts of slander. You'd often see them ignore orders, cut corners in their work, or even quit because they didn't like the new boss—or even worse, get openly hostile. If things descended to that level, staff recommendations became the last thing on the manager's mind.

"But we all work really well at Hatagaya, don't we? And our location offers a lot of different services. You don't think we'll get a manager all uncooperative like that, do you?"

"You wouldn't think so, right? But businesses are full of incompetent, petty people. And maybe they shape up later on, but it's not uncommon to see people who really make you think it'd be better if they never existed. You just can't ever be sure until they're actually there. It's the relationships between coworkers that really drive results, after all."

The atmosphere of a workplace really came down to the collected relationships between the staff. Sometimes a person deemed talentless might join a team, tangle with them a bit, and eventually mature into a good contributor. Other times, a "talented" worker would join up, attempt to boss around the crew, generate discord, and send sales tanking. Of course, sometimes you found that golden child who was talented enough to take good sales and make them even better—but most of the time, useless people stayed useless, unconsciously wrecking the location until they finally disappeared.

The only thing anyone was really sure of? Once Kisaki was gone, the Hatagaya Station MgRonald would never be the same again.

"Along those lines... I'm worried that Marko is a little too oriented with the way I do things. He's broad-minded enough to work with a new manager, but he's kind of got this obstinate passionate streak, too, you know? He doesn't like it if something's illogical or doesn't make sense."

Kisaki had a good eye for her crew. Maou really did tend toward logical, reasonable answers to solutions. It made it hard to believe he was a bloodthirsty Devil King at all.

"Plus, he's a shift supervisor. I'm worried he's going to try reconciling the new system with what he knew back when I was around. If he winds up clashing with the new manager, depending on how she sees him, he may not get another chance at managerial training for quite a while. Which, you know, if another manager transfers in, that changes things...but Marko doesn't have that much time, does he?"

""Huh?""

"It's about that time where he needs to start thinking about a life plan. Your early twenties isn't too early at all to worry about that. I just don't think it's realistic for him to stay holed up at MgRonald for the rest of his life."

""Ahh!""

"What?"

Considering they were just discussing their assault on heaven and the time frames involved, Chiho and Emi, naturally, both thought Kisaki was talking about that at first. Once they realized the earthly truth, they both nodded.

""N-no, uh...""

"The ages of twenty-two, twenty-five, and twenty-nine are extremely important watersheds in your life. That's especially true with Marko— part-timing this whole way instead of going to college. If he gets too attached to his first dream of being a MgRonald full-timer, he could end up wasting the best years of his life."

Exactly what entailed the best years of Maou's life was up for debate, but it wasn't worth telling Kisaki that.

"I mean, I know I'm not one to talk. I love my job right now, but I was so anxious during my job hunt that I immediately compromised on MgRonald the moment I got the offer. I guess I'm not exactly the world's best motivator here."

"Huh?" Chiho was surprised to hear this. "You 'compromised' on MgRonald? I mean, I've never seen you anxious in my life!"

"They called it the employment ice age back then. It was a terrible time to be out of college and looking for a career. And it was my dream to work in restaurants, but after pondering it, I wound up going with a mega-corporation. That's why I call it a compromise. Besides, as a manager, it's kind of my job to be anxious. We got baseline sales quotas to make, after all."

Kisaki smiled a bit, recalling the past.

"You'll know what I mean in three or four years, Chi. Job hunting is scary in a different way from high school or college exams. I bet Kota's fighting for his life right now with that stuff."

It was now March, meaning that former crewmember Kotaro

Nakayama was about to start his fourth year of college. The faster firms would already start giving students informal job offers around this time, and even those who didn't formally begin hiring until the summer of senior year would be starting with things like internships, alumni visits, and the other early steps of the job-evaluation flow. It was a scary time for applicants, bombarded with information and forced to consider a future they had no idea about yet.

"And if Marko's seeking a full-time position, he's gonna have to reconsider how much he wants that pretty soon. He strikes me as the kinda guy who was doing a lot even in the blank time periods on his résumé, so he's still a level above all the other guys in his boat... but compared to the average for other job seekers his age, he's still gonna face some bias, sadly."

Kisaki was only giving them the general state of matters in the job market. It wasn't the kind of thing that'd likely goad Maou's passion and make him want to stay in Japan.

"...You think he can achieve something?" Emi couldn't help but ask. She meant nothing deep by it, inspired as it was by her previous whining at Chiho.

"Well, worst-case scenario, if he's interested, I think I can do something for him."

"Oh?"

It sounded like Kisaki really meant that. Like it wasn't just some irresponsible promise she'd forget about tomorrow.

"But I can't do anything right now, and it'll depend on him a lot, so I can't say much more about that. Anyway, I better get going. I'm on my way to work, so..."

Kisaki turned to Alas Ramus. "Sorry I didn't give you any attention."

The child meekly nodded back.

"Okeh... Chi-Sis, I want fwies!"

And maybe it was nothing very important, but it was a sheer stroke of luck that she chose to nag Chiho, not Emi.

"Didn't you just eat?"

"You want fries...?"

"Ha-ha-ha! Well, at her age, she'll want to eat her favorite stuff all the time. You can feel free to stop by, you know, if you want."

"Sure. But you're walking to work? Where do you live...?"

The park was right near the Keio train line, around halfway between the Sasazuka and Hatagaya rail stations, but Kisaki had walked in from a side road.

"Oh, you didn't know, Chi?" Kisaki turned around and pointed a finger forward. "I have an apartment in a building on that street over there."

"Whoa! That's really close!"

It'd be less than a ten-minute walk to her MgRonald. Chiho assumed she took a car or train to work, but come to think of it, she'd never seen her traveling to or from her job before.

"Do you live by yourself?"

"No, with my parents."

"Oh, really...?"

Most of the adults Chiho associated with lately were living by themselves (or some equivalent), so Kisaki living with her parents seemed novel to her. She always pictured her living alone in a chic urban condo complex or something.

"Well, if I wasn't local, I wouldn't be able to keep tabs on the local high schools my team works at."

"Oh!"

Chiho recalled how Kisaki had asked about her high school during her job interview.

"I know Marko has a lot to think about, but you probably have to start thinking about exams, too, don't you, Chi? Better keep an eye on that—and everything else around you. When it comes time to move, move fast."

"R-right... I'll keep that in mind."

"Now, for real this time..."

Chiho watched Kisaki briskly walk away, a hand to her chest in a gesture of surprise.

"Well, that sure scared me."

"Was it really that scary?"

"It's surprising enough if you see someone from work in real life, you know? And she lives right near here..."

"Oh, maybe so. The fact that the Devil King lives in Sasazuka kind of inoculated me to that long ago."

"Yeah..."

Chiho could already feel her shock rapidly subsiding.

✳

Kisaki had mentioned that she'd stop by the MgRonald one more time after the lunch rush, but Emi never did see her before the end of her own shift. Her missing presence was likely why they were never haunted by the wailing spirit of Sariel that day; apart from Maou running on a fraction of his usual energy, it turned out to be a pretty typical shift.

Since yesterday, Emi had wondered what Kisaki meant by "I think I can do something for him." She suspected—and she was pretty sure about this—that there was a concrete plan of action behind that statement. Kisaki liked to chat, but she couldn't say something like that without intending to back it up. There was something in her mind that led her to believe she could lend a hand in Maou's life. Emi didn't know what—but it'd be much better for Maou if Kisaki had something envisioned for him, rather than if he tried for a full-time job at some other company that he didn't even want.

'Why am I thinking about this...?"

And the reason it would be better for him was, of course, because Maou missing out on a full-time job created the danger that humans and demons could go back to their old habits on Ente Isla. There *was* that danger, but for some reason, Emi was connecting it directly to Maou's work prospects. The career of her rival for all time shouldn't matter, but if she didn't worry about it, it could threaten peace across the world. She had to support him. The whole dilemma would be sad if it wasn't so chaotic.

'This is so stupid."

Shaking off these useless thoughts, Emi took out her smartphone.

She told Maou she was staying at Suzuno's place without actually asking her first, so she needed to do that real quick. The screen read "March 12" at her. Emi looked back at Maou and snickered.

"He's not thinking of doing something, is he?"

White Day, the day in Japan where men traditionally give chocolate to women in return for the gifts they'd received on Valentine's Day, was March 14. Last month, Maou had received a worrisomely enormous collection of chocolate from his demon and human cohorts, most notably Suzuno and Chiho. They didn't manage to eat it all, of course. It made Emi wonder how long chocolate stayed edible—but then, all Chiho taught the demons was how to melt retail chocolate blocks into simple molds. If they were kept in a cool, dark place, they might get harder or a bit oily, but that shouldn't affect the quality for a while.

But White Day wasn't waiting. And if every day of your life was busy, a month had a way of passing by in a flash.

"I doubt he prepared at all..."

If Kinanna hadn't shown up, would he have thought about doing something in the past week? Even without the lizard, the fallout from his rejection might've made it impossible anyway. Actually, was he still in contact with that lady who gave him the really expensive chocolate package during training?

"I doubt Chiho and Bell would care. They know the kind of shape he's in. But I wish he'd do something for Alas Ramus, at least."

As she waited for a walk sign on the street corner, she looked to her left, a hundred or so feet to the next stoplight. Almost a year ago, she had been reunited with her nemesis at that intersection.

"I bet Acieth's gonna whine about it, too. Maybe I should say something to him."

If Emi went back in time and told herself that she'd be working at the same place, in the same town, as the man she swore to kill, worrying about his career path and whether he prepared for White Day, how would past Emi respond?

"This is like..."

Smiling a little to herself, she tapped the "Call" button on her phone as she watched the walk sign turn on.

"…We're a real married couple, huh."

Ten or so minutes later, Villa Rosa Sasazuka came into view as usual. Emi breathed a sigh of relief. Depending on what Kinanna did, she honestly expected to be greeted with a pile of rubble.

She went up the stairs, not seeing or hearing anything unusual. First, she knocked on the door to Room 202.

"Emilia? Alas Ramus and Kinanna are sleeping, so keep it down," Suzuno said quietly.

The door opened.

"…Oh, Chiho? And Acieth?"

"Good evening, Yusa! I'm staying over tonight, too."

"Hello, Emi! I hope you are doing well!"

Chiho was wearing an apron, a fetching smell emanated from the apartment, and Acieth was already hard at work snacking on a plate piled high with cookies. Maybe they'd changed tactics and bribed Kinanna with some sweets? Removing her coat, Emi sat by the futon in the corner Alas Ramus slept on and observed the kitchen. The counter was lined with chocolate chips, food coloring spray, and other baking necessities.

"Why are you baking at this time of night?"

"We're experimenting a little."

"And I am taste tester!"

Emi could see that from a mile away but still smiled and nodded stiffly.

"We actually just finished this batch. Wanna try some?"

They looked like regular round cookies. Taking one, Emi spotted the faint aroma of butter—a dangerous temptation pre-bedtime.

"This is good. But really, why this all of a sudden? Are you giving them to Kinanna?"

They couldn't have been doing this simply to feed Acieth. Kinanna's upkeep seemed like the most likely reason, but Chiho's response went beyond anything Emi could imagine.

"It's almost White Day, so…"

"Huh?"

"Considering we were the ones who started this," Suzuno explained as she sampled a few of the burnt and misshapen cookies from an earlier batch, "we can hardly ignore how things are right now, can we?"

"Yeah, I was the one who taught the demons that White Day is for giving back. It'd be mean to drum up their expectations and leave them empty-handed, so I thought we could bake these for the demons."

"Oh…"

Emi stared blankly at Chiho's rapidly moving hands.

"Of course, this is only for demons!" Acieth insisted. "I will make him give good, expensive sweets to me, and Chiho, and Suzuno, and my big sister! He must spend a thousand more yen, all the days he is late!"

She was proving to be quite the loan shark.

"By the way," Suzuno casually added as she watched the evening news, "did he ever pay back the gift he received from that woman during training?"

"That's a different issue," countered Chiho, her back turned.

"Oh, and Emilia, we gave Alas Ramus a few cookies after dinner as well. It would be mean to a child, after all, baking all these and denying her a single one. So bear that in mind."

"…Sure. Thanks."

Chiho, Suzuno, and Acieth weren't just worried about how Maou would approach White Day—they assumed he'd have nothing, and they were taking action to cover for him. Chiho, in particular, had the demons make chocolate to help forge deeper bonds between them and Maou; now she was on Maou's side, making cookies to repay their efforts. Over in a corner, Emi even saw a bag from a hundred-yen shop, filled with what looked like gift wrap.

It made everything she muttered to herself on the way home seem incredibly embarrassing now.

"…!"

'Yusa?"

'What is it, Emilia?"

'You have the hunger? Eat more!"

But none knew what made Emi bury her face in her hands just then.

✳

As it turned out, Kisaki made it back to MgRonald just after Emi left.

'Ugh, that meeting went on forever! Sorry I'm late. The ten PM crowd's all gone, I assume. How'd it go today?"

'About the same as always," replied Maou. "No real trouble."

'Oh? That's good." Kisaki checked the clock. "You know, Marko, I got a text from Kota today."

'Kota?"

Maou looked up at the unexpected name. Kisaki paused. She knew full well what her words would mean to him.

'It sounds like he got an offer."

'He did?! That's fast! He's still technically a junior, isn't he?!"

'It *is* fast, but not unusually so. Plus, he was already in the whole internship system and stuff. So that's one down for him, at least. He's still courting his first choice, so he's staying on the job hunt a while longer."

'Oh, yeah?"

'Yeah."

'But that's still good news, isn't it?"

Kisaki raised an eyebrow.

'I mean, most of the time," he stammered, "you never hear what happens to someone after they leave. I'm glad things are going well for him."

'Yeah. Say, Marko…"

'Yes?"

'Are things calming down for you yet? I still wanted to treat you to dinner."

"Oh! Um, tonight should be fine... Do you mind if I call home first?"

"No problem. But if you can't... Sorry to sound pushy, but I really want another chance to talk to you sometime, so."

"Oh? Um, sure. Gotcha."

It was rare for Kisaki to be so bold like this. But for now, he'd need to text Suzuno and Emi after work to make sure he could be a little late.

"Ugh... That stupid lizard."

It felt a bit too much like a man calling his patient wife to ask whether he could join his coworkers out drinking. He grumbled about it a bit as he changed and sent the texts. He received responses promptly.

"That's all right. But not too late, okay?"

"Understood. Feel free to spread your wings a little, now and again."

They were both so kind about it that it made him sick. That, and for some reason, Chiho sent him a text at almost the same time.

"Don't worry about us here! Camio's doing better. He walked around the apartment a little tonight."

It was followed by a photo of Camio doing a little wingspread pose in front of the box with the sleeping Kinanna. If Chiho was there this time of night, she was presumably sleeping in Suzuno's apartment. He assumed she'd be all right with Emi and Suzuno there should something happen, but...

"I'll try to wrap this up as soon as I can."

But Maou, not quite sure why Kisaki wanted to see him so bad, still felt nervous. It had been a while since his rejection. Considering she just told him about Kotaro Nakayama's offer, it couldn't have been about that. Kisaki wasn't the type of person to rehash old debates that were long past being solvable.

It was now past the closing hour. Maou went out to clean up the street in front of the entrance.

"Why's it so bright out? ...Huh?"

And there he saw a Buddhist statue. A far cry from the wailing ghoul of yesterday, *this* Sariel statue had pure, unclouded eyes. The brightness was because his eyes were lit up—literally, as opposed to the eerie aura of the other day.

So Maou whapped him on the head to make him stop.

"What the hell, man? ...Ow! You're hot! Is that holy energy?! You're glowing, dude! Everyone's gonna see you!"

"Ah... Maou."

But Sariel's eyes and face remained in their pure form, looking straight up at Maou.

"Yes... Indeed, I am at a loss. At a loss, but at the same time, I am taken by a vision of pure happiness."

"What the hell're you talking about?!"

Maou could understand if the news of Kisaki's transfer sent him into depression. But now, like a purified holy statue, he was standing motionless in front of MgRonald. No matter what he did, he had a knack for bothering people.

"Something up, Marko?"

"Huh? N-no, um..."

As before, Kisaki shouted at him from inside. It only seemed to intensify the light from Sariel, as Maou gave him a sideways glance.

"Was Sarue out there?"

"What? Y-yeah, uhh..."

"Oh, he's already here? I invited him."

"You did?!"

This was such a surprise, Maou found himself shouting right in front of the entrance.

"Sorry I didn't tell you, but he's joining us tonight. Tell him we'll be just a bit longer, all right?"

It was a massive surprise, but it certainly explained Sariel's new awakening. Back when his ban from the Hatagaya Station MgRonald was lifted, he was elated, purified, to the point where he almost ascended to heaven. If Kisaki had not only spoken to him, but invited him to dinner, it must've been like heaven moved itself down to Sariel's doorstep.

"Maou?"

"Yeah…?"

"I… What should I do? What should I say to her?"

"I dunno? You never seem to have trouble talking her damn ear off. Why're you freaking out over going out with her?"

"I… I feel unprepared. Now that the moment has finally come, it's like my brain has shut off on me."

Even an angel, presumably alive for thousands of years, got tongue-tied when the woman of his dreams spoke to him.

Maou ignored Sariel—still glowing and now nervously looking at his watch—and went back to closing duty.

"I have even less of an idea what's about to happen…"

He already had little idea why Kisaki had invited him to dinner. But if Sariel was coming along, he was totally lost.

"Okay, all set. Ready?"

"Y-yes!"

Once they were done, Kisaki and Maou left through the front door, Sariel still an unmovable statue. He had managed to wind down the glowing, somehow.

"So like I said, Maou here will be joining us. Thanks for taking the time for this."

"The—the pleasure is mine!"

"…"

He didn't know what would happen. But he said he'd go, and that meant he'd be sharing a table with Sariel. No matter what happened, he was be obliged to treat the man with respect as "Mr. Sarue from Sentucky Fried Chicken." He wasn't looking forward to it—at all—but soon they were through the entrance at the usual *izakaya*.

"Sorry to keep you out so late."

"N-no, no!"

Was this really the same man who heartily sang his original love and passion-filled poems to the general public inside MgRonald? Sariel, seated across the table from Kisaki, was like a frozen stone, one apt to shatter if you hit it with a hammer.

"Mr. Sarue? Are you okay? Would you like something to drink?"

Maou, unsure how to act, presented him with a drinks menu.

"I-I'll get a beer!!" he replied, ignoring it. Maou wondered if alcohol was a good idea in his condition.

"Yeah, maybe I should have a drink, too. It's been a while. Maybe *shochu*?"

She started thumbing through the menu. Maou, feeling self-conscious about having a plain oolong tea, decided to join in for one round.

"And I'll have an oolong...highball."

After making the order, he realized this was just the second time he had tried alcohol in Japan. The first time was at a little welcome event held a while after MgRonald hired him. Kisaki was there then, too—and really, he didn't remember how it tasted.

So Kisaki ordered the three drinks for the table, along with a few dishes to share. Due to the late hour, the drinks all came first—Sariel's draft lager, Maou's oolong-*shochu* iced tea, and Kisaki's straight *shochu*.

"Well, here's to another day in the books. Thanks for coming out, you two."

At her signal, everyone raised their glasses. Sariel, with his medium-sized stein, was obliged to hold it with both hands to keep from shaking too much.

Maou took a drink of his highball. A cool yet warm sensation streaked down his throat. Kisaki watched him as he enjoyed it, warmly smiling, head propped up with her arm.

"To be honest with you, I wanted both of you to drink a little bit tonight. If I said something stupid, I wanted to be able to laugh it off as the alcohol talking. Thanks for taking my invite on such short notice."

"Sure..."

"The—the honor is mine!"

Kisaki dove into a small bowl of edamame, taking occasional sips from her drink as she spoke.

"I know it's late, so I'll get right down to business. As you know, I'm transferring to a new job at the start of the fiscal year on April 1.

The Hatagaya Station location's gonna have a new manager, and I hope both of you will get along with her..."

"Of—of *course* I will!" said Sariel, despite the concept turning him into a vengeful wraith on the streets when he first heard the news.

"But that doesn't matter tonight. There's actually a favor I want to ask from you both. That's why I invited you."

"Y-yes?!"

"A favor—? Whoa, you're gonna break the glass with that death grip."

Maou thought he could hear the stein cracking in Sariel's hands. He didn't know his own strength, apparently.

"I'm twenty-seven now."

"I am aware, yes!!"

"Huh? ...Oh."

Maou wondered what kind of crime Sariel committed to know that piece of info. Then he recalled that his boss was Kisaki's friend from when they were young.

"And the department I'm transferring to is more of an internal home-office thing, but once I work there three years, I'm thinking about leaving the company."

""Huh?""

Maou and Sariel both let out surprised yelps. In three years, Kisaki would be thirty—right when you entered the main earning period in your career.

But the truth dawned on Maou then:

"You're gonna go independent?"

Kisaki nodded. She dreamed of having her own bar and restaurant, and both Maou and Sariel knew she was taking baby steps toward that dream. But hearing that resolve straight from her mouth was still a surprise to them. Honestly speaking, Kisaki was getting one killer promotion. It put her on the track to big things in the MgRonald Corporation. And now she was talking about doing away with that stability...

But why was she telling them?

"Yeah. And I suppose you could call this headhunting." She belted down her glass of *shochu*. "Marko, Sarue... Three years from now, I want to hire you."

The night wind felt good against Maou's flushed cheeks—an unfamiliar sensation. He was on his way home, pushing Dullahan II along. The shocking offer had paralyzed his mind; he still wasn't sure how to parse his feelings about it.

The city around him was quiet, as if it was watching over him. Villa Rosa Sasazuka, too, was serene. The lights were off in Room 201 and 202—no unusual sounds or anything. Quietly, so as not to wake anyone, Maou went through the door.

"<Ah, Satan, you have returned?>"

"Whoa!"

Kinanna's voice pierced the darkness, a pair of reptilian eyes shining a fluorescent green in the air. Maou's pulse, already quickened by the alcohol, began to race.

"<Y-you're awake? Why are you out?!>"

"<Out? Don't be silly,>" the composed lizard replied. "<This is not outside at all!>"

He was seated in the middle of the room, the box inside his holy-energy cage ripped to shreds. Next to it, Camio was gently dozing as always. The sight frustrated Maou a little. The chicken could be eaten at any moment, and yet, he was chill enough to sleep?

"<I will always be inside this burrow. I will never renege on my promise to you.>"

"<This burrow? That's a mean way to put it... Wait.>"

He steeled himself, assuming Kinanna was talking nonsense again. Then he noticed something else.

"<I will always be here, so as not to renege on the pact within my body. I will only move from here when chaos rules the world anew.>"

"<Um... Where is 'here'?>"

"<What? Have you forgotten, Satan? After all the tears you shed, begging me to forgive you?>"

"<S-sorry... I've also had my hands full lately.>"

He had to play along.

"<Hmph. Very well. Do not worry. When Legoon visited my burrow earlier, I taught *him* a lesson he'll not soon forget!>"

"<Well, ah, good work...>"

"<But if Legoon has found where my burrow is, then has Camuinica been dispatched?>"

"<Well, you know, uhh, he has a son...>"

It felt strange, referring to the father figure who'd raised him as someone else's child. But he did anyway—to great effect.

"<What? A son?! Then we must care for him! So there is another generation... Ah, this is excellent news! We must care for him, so the nefarious Legoon never finds him! But I do not appreciate how the Nothung is not being maintained. Oh, if only I could move from here, I would come right over to celebrate—but alas, it is not to be. Please, give Camuinica my warmest regards!>"

"<I will. He'll be glad to hear that.>"

Maou took off his shoes and sat next to Kinanna, keeping the lights off to avoid startling him.

"<Say, Kinanna, do you know where the Astral Gem is?>"

It sounded like, for the first time over the past few days, he had awakened some Gem-related memories. Maou tried hooking some of them, figuring he had nothing to lose.

"<Hmm? I am inside, in case the worst happens. I do not know. *You* are the one who made the burrow that way.>"

"<Oh, did I? That's right.>"

What did he mean by that? What did being inside mean here?

"<What, are you tired? You could never defeat Legoon like that. You became our chieftain after overwhelming us with your sharp-tongued words. Now is no time for weakness.>"

"<...My apologies. All these things are happening at once, and it's just a lot for one demon to deal with.>"

"<I see! And that is what brought you to me? Yes, I imagine it is. What with young Camuinica and all... Yes, yes...>"

Kinanna raised his voice in self-satisfaction. Then he blinked and looked around the room.

"<But why is it this dark?>"

"<Huh? Because it's night right now...>"

"<Night? Of course not. There would be stars in the sky at night.>"

"<What?>"

"<The sun shines in the sky. The blue star twinkles. The star that brings such pure, kind light to my burrow.>"

"<I...see...>"

He must have been talking about the sky back in the demon realms. But never, in all his years there, did Maou see stars in that realm's skies. It was always red, day and night, covered in thick clouds kicked up by the strong winds. And what blue star was this?

"<Wait! Is Legoon behind this?!>"

"<N-no. I walked all the way here, but there was nothing outside. It was perfectly peaceful.>"

"<Was it? By the way, Satan, what happened to Camuinica?>"

"<Um...>"

"<I have not seen him lately. I must sharpen his Nothung...>"

"<Don't worry. Camuinica's busy raising his son right now.>"

"<What? He has a son?! Ahh, finally, a new generation!>"

"<Mm-hmm. I go check up on him every now and then, but he's focused on that since Legoon isn't coming anytime soon.>"

"<I see, I see! But that's no reason to let that sword go unsharpened! Tell him to visit me once things settle down, if you could...>"

The conversation was starting to loop, but Maou patiently stuck to it. By the time Kinanna finally exhausted himself and fell asleep, the night sky was starting to lighten in shade.

Looking down at the snoring lizard, Maou prepared to sleep himself. The tatami-mat floor was still wrecked, so he laid some cardboard on the floor to keep from damaging his new futon, yawning the whole way.

Then there was a small knock on the door. He opened it, only to find a sleepy-eyed Emi.

"Huh? Emi? You…"

"Finally done, huh? You were talking that whole time?"

"Yeah, sorry. Did I wake you?"

"No. Sorry, but I was sleeping just fine through it. But when I woke up and noticed you'd stopped, I thought something might've happened."

"Oh… Yeah, he just fell asleep a moment ago. That was after I was out drinking, so it wasn't so bad."

"Were you out late?"

"No, I was back here a little past one…"

Maou looked down at his watch. It was almost five.

"I'll watch him. You can sleep a little."

"…I will. Thanks."

With Maou's nod, Emi entered the apartment, noticing Kinanna sprawled out in the middle of the room like it was his reserved spot.

"Whoa! Why's he out?!"

"I dunno. Can you restrain him?"

"I guess…but I don't want to wake him up. I'll figure something out if he does."

"Thanks."

Maou went back to his futon, tossing the small, wrecked cardboard box in Emi's direction.

"I don't have any, like, cushions or anything, so sit on that if you want. I can't pay for your clothes if you rip them on something."

"You really need to apologize to your landlord."

"I can't right now. He might just rip this place apart again. I will when it's all over."

His back was turned to Emi. His answers weren't exactly forward-thinking, either.

"What did you talk about with Ms. Kisaki?"

With Emi here, Maou was now fully relieved of his duty, and his guard was completely down. Emi had mixed feelings about his attitude, but she asked anyway, wondering what motivation Kisaki would have to ask him out.

"...Ahh..."

Maou stopped for a moment.

"I think some of the meat Chi and Suzuno cooked up is in the freezer. If the lizard wakes up and acts all hungry, give that to him."

"Right, right... Good night."

He was so tired that everything must've been a pain to him. Figuring she could ask him again later, Emi meekly sat down on the cardboard, reaching for her smartphone to kill the time. Maou, Kinanna, and Camio. Three demons, exhausted and sleeping—and she was guarding them. It made her feel incredibly out of place. She smiled a little about it.

"We talked," Maou said, his back still turned, "about where my starting point is and stuff."

"...Huh?"

It took time for her to realize he was answering her question from before. It sounded like this was something important.

"What do you mean?"

"...Zzz...zzz..."

"Hey?"

No answer. Leaning over, she found Maou fast asleep with a pained expression. She stared blankly at him for a moment.

"...Well, thanks," she said, standing up and leaning against the kitchen counter.

"Mmh... Emilia...*bok*..."

Then, with hardly a break, Camio woke up.

"Oh, morning. I just picked up guard duty from the Devil King. He got out of his cage again, so keep quiet. I'll get 'im if he wakes up."

"Oh, dear. My thanks to you. Ahh, nothing good has happened to me in my times in Japan, *churrrr*..."

Emi smiled. She knew this was actually an arch-demon, but the mannerisms of a large black chicken were just too weirdly cute to her.

"Are your wounds better?"

"I'd like to say they are fully healed, but it is hard to tell for *churrrr* until my demonic force returns. That will be difficult around Kinanna. *Peep.*"

"Ah. Well, at least you're feeling well."

She was glad to see a demon safe. She expressed that emotion in words. There, in the quiet early morning, she contently watched the back of the sleeping Devil King.

"Hey, Camio? What do you think the Devil King's starting point was?"

"*Peep?* Starting point?"

"He was talking about that before he fell asleep. He went out to eat with his boss last night, but they were talking about something related to their starting points as people."

"Hmm. Starting points. I *peep* wonder. I am not sure myself. I imagine one reason my liege sought to unite the demon realms was the annihilation of the Blacksheep clan, but *cheep* certainly that was not the only spark."

"Blacksheep?"

"The name of the clan His *peep* Demonic Highness was born in."

"Blacksheep... Is that the name of a particular species of demon, like the Malebranche?"

"Indeed. Malacoda, the Southern Great Demon General, is from the Bluehorn clan. Alciel of the East is of the Iron Scorpion. And I am a *peep* Pájaro Danino."

"I think I've heard the name Bluehorn before. What about Lucifer?"

"Among us, Lucifer *peep* is known as an *outcast*. The term refers not only to Lucifer but to any demon who is the last or among the last of his kind, due to being annihilated or subjected to mutation. His Demonic Highness himself may be an outcast by this point, in fact."

"An outcast...?"

The last, or among the last, of his kind. That meant the Blacksheep clan was gone.

"Why did the Devil King become the Devil King...?"

There, for the first time, Emi wanted to know about the past of the demon called Satan, someone who had always been Devil King for as long as she'd been alive.

Maou finally started moving his achy joints a little past eleven, the sun now high in the sky.

He woke to find Suzuno, not Emi, in his room. There was now also a wooden crate, much sturdier than the cardboard box Camio called home, and Kinanna was sealed inside it.

"Whoa, you didn't nail that to the wall, did you, Suzuno?"

"I—*peep*—I warned her it might be a bad idea," Camio sheepishly stated. Suzuno, on the other hand, looked proud.

"This apartment is already a disaster area," Suzuno said. "Another nail or three will not change matters. We should have done this from the very beginning. With a crate, I can cast a spell meant for sealing up a treasure chest, not physically binding a creature down. This way, he can only annoy us with the sounds he makes banging around in there. It should help you sleep better at night."

"Yeah... Maybe, but... Where's Emi?"

"You saw her early in the morning. She did not sleep much last night, so she is having a nap in my apartment. Chiho told me your shift begins in the afternoon today? If you want something to eat, I can prepare it for you."

"...Yeah, if you got something, I'd appreciate it. God, that drinking last night must've dehydrated me. I'm so thirsty."

"You, drinking? How novel."

"The kinda situation I was in, I *had* to drink to withstand it," Maou said as he filled and gulped down a cup of water from the kitchen tap. "I only had two drinks, too...but I feel so heavy. This must be what a hangover's like."

"Likely, you simply have a low tolerance. Let me see your left hand."

"Hmm? ...Ohh?!"

He lifted up his palm. Suzuno jabbed a single finger into the middle. There was a shock, followed by a refreshed feeling that coursed across his body, freeing him from the dull alcoholic haze.

"Wow, that was great. What was it?"

"A spell that energizes the flow of water inside you and dilutes the alcohol. It has little effect if you ingest a great deal of it, but the spell is simple enough that it does no harm to a demon."

"Yeah, I feel a lot better. But that's kind of a niche spell, isn't it? When do you ever use it?"

"Many are the clerics among us who cannot drink or are vulnerable to its effects. But we cannot perform our divine ceremonies and rituals and only *pretend* to drink our holy wine."

Maou blinked at this. Talk about the perfect solution to a common (?) problem.

"A lot of demand in the industry then, huh?"

"I...hesitate referring to the Church as an industry."

"I mean, to the average person, a spell like that would make no sense, but if you're 'in the business,' so to speak, you'd know exactly what it's for, that sort of thing."

Suzuno gave Maou a funny expression. Something had inspired him, and it wasn't just the anti-hangover spell talking.

"Oh, speaking of, sorry about showing up so late yesterday."

"Not at all. Emilia and Chiho were here with me. And you could hardly afford to turn down a proposal from Kisaki, so close to her transfer."

"I appreciate that. I think last night gave me more insight on the future."

"Insight?"

It might have been Suzuno's imagination, but she felt some of the light from before returning to Maou's eyes.

"Listen, do you have any urgent business in Ente Isla today?"

"What? I could sleep here tonight if need be, but what's the matter?"

"In that case, today... Well, actually, tomorrow morning, I have something I want to talk about with you, Emi, and Chi. I'd prefer tonight, but I can't have Chi sleeping over here two nights in a row."

"All right. Should I tell them?"

"Yeah. If you can, I'd like to get Ashiya and Urushihara here, too. And Laila and Acieth while I'm at it."

"Is this a major undertaking you are planning?"

"Not major in my book, no, but something that'd probably piss you all off if I did it without warning, so I wanted to talk about it. Ugghhh, I'm so tired."

With a hefty yawn, Maou got up, the vibrant force extending off his back like an aura. Suzuno watched him as he looked at the morning sun.

"Well, if you feel better, then all is well."

The way he was talking, he'd never reveal it until everyone was there, no matter how much she prodded him. Suzuno moved on to cooking breakfast.

"Maou, is it me, or…is the whole Sentucky building glowing?"

Chiho, fresh from school and about to start her shift, felt obliged to whisper the question into Maou's ear, so none of the other crew could hear her.

"Yeah. It already was when I came to work."

"That early…? Doesn't anyone else see it?"

"I'm not sure. Maybe, if they're looking out for it."

"Um, are you okay with that?"

"No, but I think you could still play it off as an optical illusion or something. Good thing we're on a well-lit city street even at night, huh?"

"What do you think happened to Sariel…?"

If something supernatural was happening to Sentucky Fried Chicken, Chiho surmised Sariel had to be the cause of it. She was right.

"Well, you know how Ms. Kisaki invited me out last night?"

"Yeah."

"Sariel came with us."

'Huh?"

"Yeah, she invited him."

"*Whaaat?!!*"

If someone else had said that to Maou, he'd react the same way.

"Did—did—did Sariel finally use his angel magic to take over Ms. Kisaki's mind or something?"

"No, nothing like that. I know it's easy to think that, but no."

Maou could see why Chiho needed assuaging. Until Kisaki started talking, he had zero idea why she'd do something like invite Sariel to eat with her. He doubted Sariel did, either. And when she originally said "I want to hire you" to them, neither understood at all what she meant at first.

＊

"Marko, Sarue... Three years from now, I want to hire you."

Maou and Sariel froze, blinking helplessly.

"Hire us?"

"I—I am not sure what you mean..."

"I mean exactly what it sounds like. You both know my dream, right?"

"Y-yes, the bar and café..."

"I'm saying, when I'm ready to manage that, I want you both to help me. We can discuss compensation later, but I want to get a company going and hire you on in relatively quick order."

"I'll do it."

Realizing Kisaki was serious, Sariel bit on it like a Venus flytrap whose feelers were set off by a juicy bug—a reflex, his own volition playing no part in it. Maou gave him a slap on the head for it.

"What was that for?!"

"Dude, you... Er, I mean, please give it some thought, Mr. Sarue."

"I don't need to! What reason do I have to hesitate?!"

"If you don't, that's fine. But unlike me, you're a full-time employee at Sentucky, Mr. Sarue. Are you sure you should commit to a new job that quickly?"

"All the thinking in the world won't help you if you don't act on it. And *all* my decisions are snap decisions!"

"That's not what I mean! And what about you, Ms. Kisaki? Hiring Mr. Sarue? Are you trying to doom this café from the start?!"

Maou brought a hand to his forehead, as if dealing with a migraine.

"Maybe hindsight is twenty-twenty and all, but you know, I really do trust Sarue."

"Trust him *how*?!" Maou blurted out.

Kisaki snickered back. "Well, he's never gonna stab me in the back, right?"

"Of course I won't!"

"No, um… All right, probably not, but…"

"And yes, he sometimes says and does strange things, but he's always a perfect gentleman to women."

"Thank you for saying that!"

"I have a feeling we don't share the same concept of a perfect gentleman, Ms. Kisaki."

"I've noticed something over the past few days. To put it nicely, Sarue is a perfect gentleman. To put it poorly, he's a loser."

"That is an honor to hear!"

"Shut up! Are you gonna react that way to everything she says?! Ms. Kisaki, what are you talking about?!"

Now Sariel was in his element. Shedding all the nervousness, he was back to his usual outlandish behavior. Kisaki paid it no mind.

"Considering how he showers me with praise every single day, he's never laid a hand on me, has he?"

"Laid a hand…? Well, technically speaking, no, but…"

"And he draws a very clear line between business and private matters. Besides, the Sentucky in Hatagaya's a good sales performer."

"It is…?"

Maou recalled Kawata telling him how Sariel had attempted to apply for a part-time job at the MgRonald across the street.

"And I've realized that I'm totally capable of fending him off, too.

So think about it. He adores me, he's a faithful worker, and he's easy to handle. You don't see people like that too often."

"You truly think so much of me... Ahh... Am I dreaming?!"

'Don't you get it? She's telling you you're a useful idiot."

As sorry as most people would be for Sarue in this context, the man himself was in a state of abject joy, so Maou laid off.

"...Well, whether I agree with you or not, Ms. Kisaki, I'm fine with it if you are. But don't you want to hear why as well, Mr. Sarue? Like, why us, and what your conditions are, and so on."

Kisaki smiled defiantly at the word *conditions*. She was sure she had them now. Sariel, meanwhile, shook his head violently.

"Conditions?! Ms. Kisaki is seeking my company! What more conditions would I need?!"

"That's not how I would describe it. Also, Sarue, Marko's right. I'm asking you to entertain an offer that could drastically lower the amount of money you make in your lives. So listen up. When your boss talks about labor conditions to you, you need to listen."

Sariel, suitably chastised, fell silent.

"Basically, there are two reasons. First, I want to run my own bar-café, but as it is, I would need to run the managerial side by myself, too. If I did that, I'd be lucky to last three years before I got exhausted. Running a restaurant is about a lot more than making food and drinks and serving it to customers. I need other people who can handle that for me at any time, so I can focus on other stuff. That's reason number one."

"Right. Fair enough."

"Second, I don't want to spend a lot of time and money selecting my starting staff. As I said, I definitely can't run this thing by myself—but if I want to hire part-timers, I may have to wait a while until I attract them, and frankly, I'm not gonna have the time to train them from the get-go. On the other hand, I'd gladly pay to have you on board, and I can leave the space for you to run it when I'm busy."

"Wait a minute, Ms. Kisaki! You *trust* him with that? I understand if you think he's a useful idiot, but how can you possibly trust this guy?!"

"Like I told you. Because he's deeply, inconsolably in love with me."

"That I am! And I won't let anyone beat me on that!"

"Whoa?!"

Kisaki's strange logic portrayed her in a totally different light to Maou.

"Well, all right, I'm half joking there, but..." she quickly followed up.

"I'm always one hundred percent serious!"

"Will you shut up?! Um, joking or not, that's just crazy talk. Where are you getting this from?"

"Before I say anything further, Marko, let me ask. What do you think you need to open an Italian-style bar...or a café, to keep this simple?"

"Huh? Well..." Maou thought for a moment, realizing how broad the question was when talking about management. "You have to develop a menu first. Drinks and food. Then you work out the recipes, then your wholesale prices and suppliers. Dishes and utensils. Also, you gotta find a space and get the tables and chairs for it..." A pause. "Oh, and you need a custodian, too. Then once you start getting customers, you look at the numbers, compare what sells with what doesn't, revise the menu... Then, um..."

He listed the things that occurred to him during day-to-day MgRonald operations, but nothing else came to mind. Then he noticed Sariel grinning confidently at him, nostrils flared.

"Hmph. Shallow. How shallow, Maou!"

"Huh?!"

"All you're talking about is the front-of-house operations!"

"Really?"

"You can't manage a restaurant unless you handle the back end, too, Maou. In other words, the money."

With an aggravated expression, Sariel made a circle with his thumb and index finger.

"You started by thinking about building the part of the restaurant the customers see. But that's wrong. You start managing a place by calmly, coldly checking over the cards in your hand."

His voice was calm, as if admonishing an underperforming student.

"You have a loan from the bank. You have collateral. You have your personal funding ratio when you open for business. You have a repayment plan. You have your operational budget for the time being. Cash flow. Sales goals. Plus a lot more details, but you have to calculate all these when you're launching a new location. If you don't have a full business plan with all these numbers worked out, the bank's not going to sit down with you, much less give you a loan. And if you *do* get that loan and have a budget to work with, that's when you can start thinking about what the place looks like. Though, really, you do that in parallel with the money stuff after a certain point."

Maou had learned about this in his managerial training. Why didn't he come up with that himself just now? And why was Sariel rattling this off so perfectly?

"You have to maintain your books—accounts payable, accounts receivable, expenses, salaries, taxes. You have to interact with the bank regularly. If you hire part-timers, hiring and training them is part of the job. And if you're treating it like some nondescript café on the outskirts of town, the only way that'll work is if you have roots in the neighborhood, or you're a rich businessman doing all the building and running this as a side hobby. Whether it's a bar or a café, you're dealing in luxuries. It's not a vital, life-supporting business."

"I hate to say it, but Sarue's right. The Italian bar-café concept isn't too mainstream in Japan, either."

"I don't need to tell you how accessible, cheap, comfortable chains have altered the landscape in most neighborhoods. That's the kind of scene we'd be abandoning a career-track job to wade into. You need to understand that massive businesses and pioneers used vast sums of money and time to deploy countless talented people into this business, and that's what's behind the restaurant you visit on a regular basis. If you mess up the basic weapons you need when joining the fray… Heh-heh. Maou, I don't think you have what it takes to run a location."

The words, coming as they did after his rejection, stabbed Maou like a knife. The fact that it was Sariel doing the stabbing made it sting even worse.

"If you start," Kisaki said, "by thinking about what you want the customer-facing things to look like, your budget's just going to keep ballooning. Sometimes you need to make an effort on the back end to make the front more attractive, sure, but management needs to be based in reality. It's nothing you can dive into romantic dreams over when you're talking about it. And even before I dive in, I think Sarue and I are of similar minds about this. He's the man Himeko Tanaka herself put in place to compete against me, after all."

It was high praise from Kisaki, who didn't know the truth behind how Sariel got where he was. Sariel, meanwhile, held his nose so high that his head was about to fall off.

"Like Sarue said, money gets involved with far more than just the opening. MgRonald has a single company-wide system for handling daily accounting and supply work, but if you're a single location, you gotta do all that yourself. Hiring an accountant or a tax agent costs money. You have to solve as many problems as you can on your own, or you'll run out of money. That's another thing difficult to keep up with if I'm all alone. I need to learn it all and come to grips with it as a manager. And while I do that, the difference between having a trustworthy staff on hand or not is huge."

Maou knew that back-end work was key to restaurant management, but he still didn't see how that connected to needing him *and* Sarue. If Kisaki was running the back, either one of them could handle the front.

"I was thinking about that after this transfer," Kisaki explained when he asked. "If I'm gonna do this, I want to do something big. I've built up all this knowledge in a large corporation. Why should I be content with being the queen of a little fiefdom? I don't want to use this dream simply to keep food on my table."

She'd need to keep at least one location going, of course, or there was no point. But just doing that couldn't be described as a lofty goal.

"If the business gets on track eventually, we could totally consider a second location. Then we'd have more people. And when that happens, if I have a faithful employee with managerial experience—like Sarue—I could immediately leave the location to him."

"I—I see…"

Maou had internally figured that Kisaki wanted to go independent so she could run a funky little place with a small but dedicated customer base. He was wrong. In fact, he rather haughtily said it himself at one point, didn't he? That if you aim high and fail, you'll still reach a higher point than you would if you set your goals lower?

"And when that happens, Marko, that's probably when you'll really be tested."

"What do you mean?"

"If our business expands, I'll get on the front lines less and less. You know the ideals I have about field-level work…and I think you're the only one who can keep those safe for me."

"Protect your ideals on the field… Ow!"

Maou groaned as the jealous archangel stomped on his foot underneath the table. He put up with it. He *did* kind of whack him hard on the head earlier.

"I know the approach you take to work by now. There's really not a lot of people out there who can learn and acquire new skills and techniques while they're busy with everything else. And you've got the skills, and the drive, to use the MgRonald limited menu to satisfy any customer. You like working in this business, don't you?"

"Well, I don't dislike it, but couldn't anyone do that if they tried…?"

"If they tried, yeah. But not many can do that. If they could, we wouldn't have this entire industry of certification courses and classes on how to improve your cooking and so on."

Kisaki looked Maou in the eye.

"Yes, a lot of people are hard workers. But not many of them truly love their work from the heart, trying to improve on their own volition while still on the job. I think you're one of the few people who really do. And when I say that, I'm not saying the rest of the crew is worse than you, but… You know, like I said, one reason why I have so much praise for you is that, out of the people around me, you have the most freedom in your future as a part-timer. I kind of figured internally that if I asked, maybe you wouldn't mind following me."

In a way, it was almost like she was asking him out. Out of the corner of his eye, Maou could see Sariel glaring at him, his face about ready to explode.

"For now, Sarue and I are talking strictly about the hard money aspects. You need money to build the foundation for a lot of dreams. But as I told you, working hard on the back end so you can get more romantic with the front is also important. Why am I dreaming of running an Italian bar-café, something so nonmainstream in this day and age? Well, it's because I had a starting point that made me embrace that dream."

"A starting point..."

"My maternal grandfather ran a café."

That café was in Kawagoe, Saitama Prefecture, northwest of Tokyo. Kawagoe, home to many historic buildings, was a popular place for visitors from nearby Tokyo to visit, and his café had been a cherished part of the local scene, keeping it pretty busy...apparently anyway. Kisaki had been a kid at the time, so she didn't know for sure. It was usually decently crowded when she visited, but her grandfather always saved a bar stool for her, blending up a special mix of coffee that was okay for kids to drink.

"You could smoke in there, like you could everywhere back then. When I look at the photos, it didn't seem trendy at all, inside or out. Granddad ran the bar while Grandma did the serving, so I'm sure they didn't have a lot of staff expenses. If they were both counted as full-timers, they could save on taxes that way, too."

Considering this was the starting point for her dream, Kisaki wasn't exactly gushing about the place.

"But my grandfather, standing there by the bar, just seemed so cool to me. He'd wear this starched white shirt my grandmother ironed for him with a black tie, a well-worn apron, and a perfectly kept mustache. If you looked up *coffee shop owner* in the dictionary, you'd see a picture of him there."

"So you were inspired by the grandfather you admired?"

"…Well, to be honest, I only felt that way about him after he closed it down."

"Oh?"

'My grandmother died when I was thirteen or fourteen, and when she did, it really took a toll on him. He couldn't hire someone to replace her at that point, and then he broke his hip falling down the stairs. He wound up having to close the coffee shop not even half a year after her death. But…"

But while her family worried that being bedridden and out of work would make him go downhill fast, something unexpected happened.

"All the café regulars stopped by to check on him."

He had a pretty wide customer base, including a few children brought there by their own grandparents. And the one thing they all told him was that they wanted Mr. Kisaki's coffee and tea again.

"They missed his work. What greater reward would an artisan want? And seeing that, it made *me* want to try his coffee again, too. I asked him, and he said, 'When I'm better, when I'm better.'"

Maou dreaded where the story was going for a moment. But after a lengthy recuperation, Kisaki's grandfather finally recovered and made some coffee for her.

"Using only what was there in the kitchen, he made my coffee exactly how I liked it. He used cheap beans from the local grocery store and filtered tap water. But it was great. I was shocked. It was the same beans and water Dad put in the coffee maker every day, but the taste and aroma were on a whole other level."

She asked him what his secret was. His answer: "I just know exactly how you like it, Mayumi."

"The way that he put it, people have a lot of number ones."

"Number ones?"

"Yeah. When we talk about food or drink, we subconsciously categorize them a lot—we say we like this from group A or that from group B. My grandfather knew the unique aspects of the roasts he dealt in, and he had a skill for guessing which one any given customer would like and making it for them."

As he put it to her:

"'If you literally ask them what the best whatever is, they'll universally give you the absolute number one on the market. But it's not like they eat or drink only the very best out there. You know what I mean, Mayumi—how this might be the best dish at this restaurant, but if you go to that café, you should get this instead? That's what I mean by people having lots of number ones. My job at the café was to get customers to pick their number one from my selection. It'd be far too presumptuous of me to select an absolute number one for them. I'd have them try a few different things, and if they found something they personally liked the best, that was a job well-done in my book.'

"So then I asked him what *my* number one was. And he said:

"'If someone told you what it was, Mayumi, it wouldn't be *your* number one any longer. You find your favorites on your own, so they'll be convincing to you. It's not something someone can teach you.'

"And you know, he never *did* tell me what my number one coffee was. So I started experimenting, trying to replicate what he made for me. He passed away when I was a sophomore in college, but before he did, he taught me a whole lot of things. Not, like, really tricky techniques or anything. But even now—even if I run into something I think is good—I've never run into the coffee my grandfather made for me. I really think it's something I need someone to make *for* me, if anything. So..."

Kisaki looked at Maou.

"I think you've got what it takes to re-create the starting point of my dream. And if you do, that can connect to providing my café's ideal offerings—the constant drive to give each customer the best things possible."

Ignoring the demonic death gaze from Sariel, Maou thought this over for a moment. But not a very long moment.

✳

"Wh-wh-wh-wh-wh-what was your answer?! You! What did you say to her?!"

"Whoa, Chi, what's wrong?!"

Chiho was giving Sariel a run for his money, with how intently she was staring Maou down from below.

"I-I-I-I-I mean, th-that's almost like her saying 'I want you to cook for me every day'!" Chiho went on. "That's, like, eighty percent of the way toward a marriage proposal!"

"M-marriage? What're you talking about? Nobody mentioned marriage!"

Chiho was visibly perturbed, and Maou was unsure of what to say. She understood what he meant; she really did. But was this *really* just a conversation between two people dedicated to their work?

"I know they didn't, but they might as *well* have! Anyway, what did you tell her?!"

Kisaki's choice of words alarmed Chiho, but there were more important issues at hand. The way she saw it, this was their best possibility yet for avoiding the danger Emi had brought up. Everyone knew Maou had a deep respect for Kisaki, and Kisaki had just asked for his help running a new company. When they spoke at the park, Chiho had no idea Kisaki would make Maou a full-timer through launching her own restaurant. It seemed like a trick, somehow—but outside of getting promoted within MgRonald, this was the most effective way of keeping Maou in Japan.

If he wanted to stay with a Japanese company, that would change the prospects of nearly everything else in the world. It wouldn't solve all of Emi's many concerns, but wouldn't it at least keep a lot of people around her from being sad?

But Maou simply pointed at the glowing Sentucky across the street.

"Can't you tell just from that? Sariel said yes, and I said no."

"You… What?!"

She was sure he'd say yes. Maou, expecting that, smiled.

"Three years is just too far away. Neither anyone else nor I could ever predict what I'll be doing then. If she had said next year, I would've agonized over it a bit more, but three...?"

"That... That's true, yeah."

Three years was more than an ample amount of time for the world to change. By then, whatever problems the world had after the conquest of heaven would become clear. Not even Chiho knew where she'd be by then.

"So I told her that if she still had a free slot in three years, invite me in then."

"Yeah... Wait, huh?"

"Hmm?"

"In three years...?"

"Yeah, like, if she still wanted me with her when she went independent, call me."

Chiho's eyes opened wide.

"So you'd say yes then? If she asked you in three years?"

"Well, it's Kisaki inviting me, y'know. It beats getting in a panic and taking a job someplace weird, right? I'm not exactly floored by the thought of having Sariel as a coworker, but..."

"Will—will you stay in contact with her that long?"

"Huh? I'm not gonna change my number or anything."

That wasn't what Chiho had asked. The mild-mannered man seemed totally oblivious of the concerns she and Emi had for him.

"Oh, right. Do you have time to stop by my apartment tomorrow, Chi? It'd have to be kind of early in the morning—like, eight or so."

"Um?"

"I wanted to talk about the future."

"The...?"

The future. The meaning behind that flashed through Chiho's mind in multiple layers. It made her face turn red, then blue, in alternating order. But:

"Maou, are you flirting with a coworker on the clock? That's against regulations."

Akiko appeared out of nowhere, face looking grim.

Chiho leaped up.

"Gahh?! M-M-M-M-M-M-Ms. O-O-Ohki?!"

"Hey, Aki. We're not flirting."

"You invited her to your apartment to talk about the future! Either you're flirting with her or proposing to her."

"Proposing? Not that word again... But I guess, yeah, the way I worded that..."

"Please stop, Ms. Ohki! It's nothing like that!!"

"All right, all right. Not that it matters, but the joint across the street is super-packed today, and we're not, so Kisaki's in kind of a huff. You better try finding some work to do."

"Sure thing."

"I told you, it's not like that!"

Maou grinned as a reddened Chiho looked up...to find Kisaki at the counter, reading her sales journal and growing visibly paler.

"Why...? Why are our numbers so low today...? What's happening at Sentucky...?"

Seeing her, Maou and Chiho simultaneously thought the same thing:

It's your fault, though, Ms. Kisaki...

Emi, watching Kinanna over in Room 201, had just received a rather harried call from Chiho on her phone.

"That's so like him, though, isn't it?" she said. "Not wanting you to stay two nights in a row."

"I—I have a bad feeling about this! Maou said he turned Ms. Kisaki down, and whenever he tries to assuage me like that, it's always when he's thinking of something really, really no good!"

"You read him like a book, huh?"

And Emi doubted that Maou suspected that for a moment.

"But he won't do anything too weird, will he? Not if he's having everyone come over for it."

"You—you don't think? What if he announces that once this is all over, it's back to being Devil King, so good-bye, Japan?"

"He wouldn't say that. Not at this point in time. Besides, if he said that in front of *me*, he'd have no complaints if I killed him right then."

"Maybe...but you know, Maou runs by his own weird logic a lot of the time, so...!"

"I was hoping you'd say that I wouldn't kill him, but...what would he gain by declaring that to all of us? The only one of us who'd be glad to hear that is Alciel, pretty much."

"Yeah, I think he'd be all 'How could you say that to her?' and stuff!"

"But he was normal at work today, right? So just try to be patient and not worry too much, okay?"

"O-okay... I'll try. I'll wake up at five AM tomorrow and head on over!"

"Nobody's going to be there then. Calm down. It's fine." With a light smile, Emi moved her phone to her other hand. "He only told *you* about Ms. Kisaki, didn't he? All I heard from him was to go to his place tomorrow morning, and even that was through Bell. And all he told Bell was to work out a time for tomorrow. So don't worry. He thinks a lot of you, all right?"

"No, not you, too, Yusa!"

"Not me what?"

"Never mind! ...But is it really gonna be all right?"

After calming Chiho down and chatting about a few other things, Emi put down her phone.

"...So you didn't hear anything?"

"Nothing, dudette. He told me to come back because he had something important to talk about, so I did."

"Oh. Well, good."

Urushihara was sitting on the closet shelf, legs dangling as he watched the computer on his lap. His response made Emi breathe a sigh of relief.

Back at the Ente Isla Devil's Castle, Ashiya was receiving an unusual visitor.

"Hey. You're back, huh?"

"What do you want?"

"Whoa, what kinda greeting is that? I was sittin' here waiting for you. They told me you'd be back from seeing the old lady in Phiyenci today."

It was Albert Ende, waiting for Ashiya in the throne-room tatami space.

"Laila… I told her to keep quiet," he grumbled.

"Whoa, don't blame her. She didn't tell anyone. The old lady herself contacted me."

"What? Dhin Dhem Wurs?"

Ashiya eyed Albert suspiciously. Albert just rolled his eyes back at him.

"Who else? She heard the story from Chiho and Bell at the zirga, but the only demons she met there were the Devil King and that Malebranche guy. She wanted me to confirm that it really was Alciel inquirin' about her. So I quizzed Laila about it, and—would you believe it?—she revealed that she was the intermediary between you and her. That's all."

"…I see."

Ashiya wouldn't have any way of knowing, but the monocle in Wurs's possession contained a Yesod fragment that reacted to the auras let off by people, revealing to her whether they were telling the truth. But Wurs still wanted to check with Albert about the demon knocking on her door—and she had reason to. She knew something that would eventually be known to all of Ente Isla but that Ashiya was keeping under wraps for the time being.

Albert smiled at Ashiya, as if reading his mind. "So following what I heard about, I figured I oughta wait here and chat with you a little."

"About what?"

"Alciel, have you ever heard of Vashrahma?"

Ashiya pondered this for a moment.

"The nation of warriors in the Southern Island desert?"

"Right. Down there, you have the lands of Tajah constantly fighting among themselves—the main family and all the branch domains—and Vashrahma is right in the middle of that. A neutral but military state. The fact that all the Tajah domains squabble without destroying one another is because none are stupid enough to make enemies out of Vashrahma."

"And what about that?"

Ashiya asked the question, but by this point, he knew full well what was motivating Albert to tell him this.

"Well, I happen to know a Chief Rajid from the Vashrahman army. Everyone in that nation, from their leader on down, is a warrior. I think you'll find 'em more receptive to you than most."

"..."

Ashiya glared at Albert awhile but turned away, defeated.

"I failed to account for this. It looks like Wurs trusts you more than I thought."

"The other Southern clans are still all yappin' at me about losing to Adramelech, and... Well, not just 'cause of that, but..." Albert pointed at a window behind him. "I'd like to think I know about the pain of a wandering warrior more than anyone else."

"...You think Emilia or Emeralda or Rumack would accept them?"

"Emeralda trusts my judgment. Emilia...I can't be so sure about, but we can reveal it to her later. And Rumack? Hell, I don't see how she matters in this. She's a Westerner. You'll hear from her when she realizes what you're up to, or if she thinks she's necessary. Otherwise, leave her be."

"Logical enough. But depending on how Vashrahma handles things, if Rumack comes along later and complains, we may not be able to do anything about it."

"Oops! Well, good thing I set things in motion early. Everything needs to be in balance, y'know."

Albert ran his hand across his head in a "phew!" motion.

"If you like, we could head there right now. They're just off the Fire Road. It'll sure warm you up after your visit up north."

"Sorry. Not today. I need to return to Japan soon...but I would like your help as a liaison. I will contact you about this later."

"Oh, figure out something new about that lizard with the Astral Gem?"

"Perhaps. That would be nice."

Alciel really meant that but didn't expect much. The sheer tension of Sadao Maou, the Devil King, in the message he'd sent out disquieted him more than anything.

"Wh-what is that?"

While Emi was on the phone with Chiho, Suzuno was walking through Hatagaya, stocking up on some purchases and internally worrying about the quantity of food Kinanna required. Then she noticed the Sentucky Fried Chicken. It had an aura of moonlight around it, glowing a shining yellow. And it was not a metaphor—the restaurant really was faintly glowing.

"That light... I detect a slight holy energy. What is Lord Sariel doing...?"

Despite it being well past the dinner rush, and despite the lack of any flashy new menu items or special offers, there was a line out the front door. It was unnerving. The MgRonald across the way, meanwhile, looked deserted—a sight that reminded Suzuno of times past, oddly enough.

Then a massive figure silently came up to her from behind, dwarfing her tiny body.

"It's glowing, is it not?"

"Agh?! Um, Ms. Shiba?!"

Miki Shiba was framed by the setting sun, herself a radiating ball of light—in no small part thanks to her dress, festooned with squares of crystal glass and absolutely not part of any woman's daily wardrobe. It made her look like a disco ball with arms and legs.

"I detected something strange, and Amane's been so worn down dealing with our friends from Ente Isla that I am checking on this myself...but if that's all this is, it should be safe enough to leave be."

"It—it is? Are you sure?!"

"It'd be a problem if he was deliberately using holy energy to attract customers, but that doesn't appear to be the case here. This is just the happy spirit coming from the restaurant. A power-infused light, naturally created by their hearts."

"A happy spirit...?"

It was the sort of term you might've seen in cult religions and tabloid advertisements twenty years ago. Hearing it from the talking disco ball—a *real* mystery of a woman, unlike any of those ads—made Suzuno frown.

"You know, we are not kind to those who wish ill upon the world. But we certainly would not dissuade anyone from finding happiness. In fact, I would even want to protect, and support, that happiness."

"Y-you would...?"

"And not to prod too much in your business, Ms. Kamazuki, but have you been inside this Sentucky before?"

"Er, yes. Several times."

"Ah, very good. I so rarely frequent *this* level of dining, so I am a tad curious. I thought I would go inside for a lark, but would you care to join me?"

"N-no! Um, I have some urgent shopping to take care of, and I need to return home right away!"

Unlike with Maou and his roommates, the mere presence of Shiba didn't seem like a threat to Suzuno. She just didn't want to dare venturing into a fast-food joint brimming with something as fishy as "happy spirit," which Sariel just *had* to be oozing inside.

"Ah, very well," Shiba replied, not looking too offended. "In that case, perhaps I will pick up something for Acieth, then. Ta-ta for now!"

She took her place in the back of the line, the light from her just as dazzling as from the Sentucky. And Suzuno, with a nervous gulp, found her feet (and a sneaking suspicion that doom was near) taking her toward MgRonald.

"Good evening... Oh?"

It was Maou, tending to business on the first-floor counter, who happened to spot her first.

"Suzuno? What're you doing? Did Kinanna do something?!"

Maou, seeing her storm in here with panic all over her face, feared the worst. But she shook her head violently as she clung to the counter.

"How—how are your sales today?"

"Huh?"

"How are your sales today?!"

"Wha—? What's with you?!"

What kind of pressing emergency would drive Suzuno to ask about MgRonald sales figures?

"What happened to Lord Sariel?! Something that turned Sentucky into the street's most popular eatery, I would assume!"

"Huh? Oh, uhhh, well, a few things, last night…"

"Well, right now…"

Maou froze. Suzuno appeared to have devastating news for him.

"…Ms. Shiba is in line at Sentucky."

"Oh—"

But before Maou could even let out a groan:

"What?!"

There was an explosion of invisible light. That was the only way to describe the force that expanded over all of Hatagaya, sending Suzuno's and Maou's attention upward toward the sky. The rest of the customers, as well as Kawata and Akiko, did the same.

How to explain what they saw? It was like Sentucky Fried Chicken had become the world's largest diamond, shining like a thousand moons. The light coming through the window was warm, powerful, and gentle.

"Why's it look so…solemn out there?"

"Devil King… The shrubbery outside is blooming…"

Right when Shiba presumably went through the Sentucky doors, the glorious new light from their rival made spring come to the plants outside MgRonald, making them flower like a well-tended garden.

"What were they *doing* in there?" Maou asked as the disco ball gracefully walked away, satisfied with the two barrels full of chicken in her hands.

"I think," observed Suzuno, "I am starting to see why you fear Ms. Shiba so much."

"Wh-what was that, just now?"

Chiho, feeling a wave of energy gently caressing her, looked out her bedroom window. It felt like the holy energy Emi and Suzuno wielded but with an edge that made her shiver. But right when she opened the window, her phone rang.

"Oh, who's this? ...Suzuki?"

The display bore the name of Rika Suzuki, Emi's friend.

"Hello? Chiho? You got a moment?"

"Yeah, sure...um, I think."

Chiho wasn't sure about that wave she just felt but nodded anyway.

"About tomorrow morning..."

"Huh? Tomorrow morning?"

"Yeah. Maou actually texted me this afternoon."

Maou and Rika had exchanged numbers? That was enough of a surprise to Chiho—but then again, Rika had been back and forth between Earth and Ente Isla numerous times. It wouldn't be strange if they stayed in contact, just in case something came up. It wouldn't be, but why did Maou pick today to text her?

"I was working when he sent it, though, and I didn't notice it until I got off. But I figured he'd be working right now if I called or texted him, so I thought I'd talk to you instead. Did you hear anything about tomorrow morning?"

"Hear...? Um, what did he text you?"

"It was pretty simple. Just, like, I have something important to talk about, so can you make it to Villa Rosa Sasazuka tomorrow morning? That kinda thing. He said morning but didn't give a time, so I wasn't sure what to do."

"Maou..."

Chiho brought a hand to her head. Maybe this sort of

communication was another reason why the managerial program turned him down.

"Plus, you know, I work tomorrow, so if it's like ten or something, I can't make that. But if he went to the trouble to contact me about it, doesn't it sound like he's made some huge, important decision about Ente Isla? I really want to be there for it."

Rika, with her feelings for Ashiya, was in largely the same boat as Chiho. She hadn't been involved with Ente Islan affairs for quite as long, but she cared for him and Emi nonetheless—she wouldn't want humans and demons to clash any more than Chiho did.

"He told me he was aiming for around eight."

"Oooh, that's cutting it close... I could be there for maybe an hour then, but oh, well... But hey, if they're gonna be killing that god or whatever, shouldn't they start thinking about what comes after that? I hope he doesn't keep leading us on like this when the time comes. He's the leader—he's got a responsibility to give us the facts when we need them."

"Yeah, totally..."

"Chiho?"

"Yes?"

If Chiho sounded down over the phone, Rika's voice made it seem like she was ready to fight right now.

"We're not gonna let 'em get away, okay? We gotta hang on for dear life!"

"...Pfft!"

Her words were simple but strong. Rika really was an older sister figure to her, and as such, it was a thrill to see her in action. Compared to Chiho, who tended to approach serious situations with excessive worrying, she was a force to be reckoned with. And when all the worrying in the world didn't solve a problem, it was people like her—doers, not thinkers—who would really save the day.

"Why don't we go together? I can wait for you at Sasazuka Station."

"Okay! I'll try to be there at seven fifty, all right? So let's both go to

bed early tonight! I gotta go make sure my shows get recorded! So see you later! And thanks!"

"No, um, thank you?"

"Why're you thanking me? Did I say something? Ah, well. See ya."

Rika's boundless enthusiasm was just the antidote Chiho needed. The mysterious discomfort she felt before the call was now completely forgotten.

The evening was about to end peacefully.

Emi was on Kinanna duty all day, but thanks to Suzuno's morning contributions and Urushihara coming back midway, the day passed without major incident. Camio was now much better, occasionally even keeping Kinanna occupied to give Emi a break, even if the chicken Suzuno prepared for the lizard still seemed to give him the willies.

Chiho and Rika both went to bed an hour early. Alas Ramus got to stay at Villa Rosa Sasazuka for the second night in a row, much to her excitement. Kisaki, reeling from the worst day of sales at the Hatagaya Station MgRonald during her entire tenure as manager, glumly staggered back home. Meanwhile, nobody saw Sariel at the Sentucky all day, but the customers kept on coming so far into the night that they had to close early due to running out of supplies. When Laila and Nord came to Shiba's house to pick up Erone, they found him and Acieth sleeping peacefully, the latter blissfully holding an empty SFC barrel in her hands. And Amane, sent out to pick up more after two barrels turned out not to be enough, turned into a pillar of ashes and blew away in the wind.

And:

"Y-Your, Your Demonic Highness, what is this sight I see before me?!"

"J-just calm down, Ashiya. I can explain!"

It was already past midnight when Ashiya, standing at the door to Room 201, visibly shook at the sight of Kinanna's aftermath.

"The walls, the floors, the curtains… Curse that lizard to hell!!"

"Ahhhh! Wait! Don't kill him! Don't use any demonic force! He's freakin' dangerous, I swear to you!"

"Alciel!" shouted Suzuno. "Please, you must hold back!"

"Do not stop me, my liege! Lord Camio! Whether he is an ancient demon who protected the first Devil Overlord or not, I cannot forgive this! *We* are the ones who must face up to our landlord, I will have you know! How much do you think we'll owe her for wrecking the apartment in such grand fashion?! She already bent the rules about pets for us— Ohh, if she only knew what happened... And you! Urushihara! Where did those headphones come from? I have not seen *those* before!"

"...Damn, you noticed already? What's the big deal? I've been working a lot lately, you know!"

"You may use that excuse once you've made up for the past year of laziness!"

"Ashiya! Please, calm down!" Maou protested. "Kinanna's finally fallen asleep! You don't want to deal with him awake, trust me!"

"No, my liege, this is a serious problem! If only I was here to observe you, I could have put this lizard and Urushihara in their places!"

"Whoa, are you putting me on the same level as a lizard?"

"You should appreciate the fact that I did not put you *below* him! We were not done talking yet! You ordered those headphones online, did you not? Just when I thought you've matured a little, this happens! Yes, just when I thought you've regained some of your self-awareness as a Great Demon General..."

"Yeah, yeah, sorry. Good night."

"Wait, Urushihara! Open that closet door! I am not done with you yet!"

"Ashiya, seriously, calm down! It's fine!" Maou said. "I worked a lot of hours this month, and I'm sure the landlord will understand once we explain things to her—"

"Your Demonic Highness, listen to me. Whether our identities are known to her or not, the relationship between her and us remains the same. The only difference is that instead of a management company, we are now essentially renting a space from the planet Earth itself. Do you understand me? We continue to live here out of the generosity of our landlord!"

'You don't need to blow up the scale of this *that* much...but yeah, I guess you're right about that."

"Indeed. And it is therefore inexcusable to assume we will be forgiven when we cause a disaster like this. Our landlord would be perfectly fine if we disappeared tomorrow. In this situation, we must bow to her as deeply as possible, and be as sincere as possible, as we apologize to her. That, and we must save as much restitution money as we can so we can remain in her good graces!"

"All right, all right! I'll explain everything to her, so just be patient with me tonight!"

"This atmosphere feels just like home again, my bros. I hate it."

"Urushihara, we can hear you!"

"Yeah, yeah... Oh, here's a delivery confirmation. Arriving tomorrow morning? Did I buy something else?"

"Damn you, Urushihara! Wasting our hard-earned money yet again?!"

"Oh, shut up! Go back to Ente Isla, Ashiya!"

"Never! Not if *this* is going on behind my back!!"

The verbal combat between a late-arriving Ashiya, Urushihara, and Maou continued well into the night. Emi and Suzuno, in their futons next door and listening in, looked at each other.

"...Funny, isn't it?"

"Yes."

"Zzz...zzz..."

Meanwhile, Alas Ramus was safely in dreamland, not giving any notice to the voices through the wall.

"It has not been that long, timewise, but it seems like much longer."

"If it was like this all the time, it'd show how peaceful the world is."

"Not *all* the time, I would hope. You get to enjoy this once in a blue moon. I have to endure it daily, and it grates on me. Particularly in the way we share a wall with Lucifer's closet."

"Oh, right."

Emi smiled and adjusted Alas Ramus's blanket. Suzuno did the same on her end, then sunk into her own sheets.

"But...just tonight is fine, I suppose."

The torrent of abuse streamed in from Room 201. And despite it all, that cacophony of noise turned into soothing music for Emi and Suzuno, both falling asleep before long.

❈

At eight AM the next morning, the front yard of Villa Rosa Sasazuka was unusually crowded. Ashiya, Urushihara, Emi, Chiho, Suzuno, Alas Ramus, Acieth, Rika, Amane, Laila, Nord, Erone, and Shiba—they were all there.

"So," Emi said first, "with all these people here, what's he gonna do first? And Rika joined in, too? And why're you carrying them in your arms? You gonna start a mobile zoo or something?"

Maou held Camio in his left arm and Kinanna in his right. The lizard was unrestrained, alarming Amane a bit.

"Um... Well, I thought about some other approaches, but I figured this was the best in the end. But this is important enough that I really wanted everyone to be on hand, so... Sorry to ask you all here this morning."

"That—that's fine, but... Is this really *that* important, Maou...?"

This early in the morning, and Chiho already looked like she saw a ghost. Meanwhile, Rika, standing next to her defiantly, locked eyes with Maou, clutching Chiho's hand to support her.

"Let me just say," a concerned Amane added, "depending on what you have in store for us, you know Aunt Mikitty and I may not sit by idly, all right?"

"I...can't comment on that."

"Oh, no..."

Chiho's legs were already shaking. Maou's pat response made Emi and Suzuno sharpen their eyes on him.

"Look...dude...just say it... I'm tired..."

The comment from Urushihara, standing on the top step of the stairway to keep his distance from Shiba, did little to relax the atmosphere.

"Right," Maou began, not wanting to delay things further. "Well, as some of you know already, my application for a full-time managerial position at MgRonald was turned down."

A pained Ashiya shook his head. "Ahh... A harsh truth to bear..."

"And as I know all of you are aware, our battle to free the brothers and sisters of Alas Ramus, Acieth, and Erone will begin once we obtain the Astral Gem, which we're pretty sure is here in Kinanna."

The lizard under Maou's arm started jabbering about something, but none of the non-demons in attendance understood him.

"<Shut your mouth.> So... With my initial goal of a full-time job at MgRonald off the table, I now officially have no reason to remain in Japan."

"Oh, Maou..."

"Hang in there," Rika said, holding the tearful Chiho's shoulders. "If he starts acting weird, hang on to him. For dear life."

Everyone assumed it then: Maou was saying good-bye to Japan.

"*But.* But... I just want to say, I've actually been headhunted."

Everyone was wrong. They all glared at him in silence for a moment. "Huh?" a few of them went in chorus, unnerving Maou.

"What? Guys, listen to me. I can't give a lot of details for non-disclosure reasons, but a certain party has asked me to join their inaugural staff when they start up their own company. But unfortunately, this isn't going to happen for at least another three years..."

"Why're you talking about *that*?" a confused Emi asked.

"Maou, you said you turned that down," Chiho added, the tears in her eyes receding for a moment.

"Well, I had to. That's in three years. I'm intending to beat Ignora, of course, but what if I'm killed or wounded beyond recovery? I'd feel so bad if I had to renege on my promise."

"...Oh..."

That was the reason? He'd turned it down for now because he didn't have a handle on his future yet, but he'd take it up again in three years if he was interested? Those in the crowd who knew about Kisaki's dream had no idea why Maou was bringing this up, and those who didn't were completely lost.

"So... Yeah. I can't say exactly what it is right now, but I've got different motivations going forward, so I can't give up yet on becoming a full-timer in Japan. So I'm gonna keep living in poverty here for a while."

"Maou!!"

No longer able to hold back, Chiho leaped for him.

"Whoa?!"

"*Peep?!*"

"*Squeak!*"

As Chiho hurtled toward them without concern, Camio and Kinanna panicked.

"I—I was so worried that—that you'd never come back to Japan this time... That you'd be Devil King all over again...!!"

"Ch-Chi?!"

Her noble tears continued to fall as she hugged him, paying no attention to the assorted animals in his arms. But even then, nobody was sure what Maou wanted to say here. Emi and Suzuno were relieved for a moment, but their faces were clouded with confusion immediately afterward.

And Rika was even more honest:

"...Why am I here?"

"She's right," an exasperated Amane said. "Why'd you make everyone here take time out of their busy schedules just to talk about your career plans? And this early, too?"

Maou hurriedly shook his head. "N-no! It's not like that! I just wanted to come out with that, since I know some of you were concerned... You're the one who said it, Urushihara!"

"Huh? Said what? You're blaming the audience turning against you on me?"

"You said I didn't have any reason to be preoccupied with Japan any longer! So I worried that Emi and Chi were thinking the same thing! I wanted to tell them that I still have a reason to be here! I didn't want to string Chi along, and if I kept leaving them in the dark, I was worried Emi and Suzuno would kill me!"

"Oh, come on…"

"Why did I ever swear my loyalty to you…?"

"Huh? Why're you looking at me like that?"

Both of them bore holes in Maou with their stares. He had clearly riled them.

"You're *so* awful."

"I see you had no trust in us at all."

"Th-*that's* what you're saying to me?! It—it's not like that with us, I swear!"

"…No, my liege, I question the *peep* wisdom of saying that myself…"

"Wha?!"

"…Daddy, you don't trust Mommy?"

"Maou… You know, Emi and Suzuno, they will not do the mean things to you with no reason! Have you lost your mind?"

"Is what I did so bad that *you* think I've lost my mind?! And no, Alas Ramus! Daddy totally trusts Mommy!"

"You liar," Laila said.

"Indeed," Erone added.

Nord, snickering, led Erone away. "Let's go over here for a bit, all right?"

"W-wait! Don't go away yet! I haven't gotten to the gist! That wasn't the main subject! I wouldn't ask you all here just for *that*! Listen to me till the end!"

Everyone except Ashiya and Chiho had their doubts about this.

"It—it's not like that, guys… To you, especially, Emi… I need to make something clear. If I want to beat Ignora and nail that job in three years, there's something we can't avoid any longer. I wanted to say it to you…"

"Well, go ahead," retorted Emi, not expecting this to be anything important, either. "Say it."

Maou placed Camio on the ground and let go of Chiho, as if preparing to make the announcement of his life.

"Based on what Kinanna's told me, it looks like—for the time being—we haven't quite reached the Astral Gem yet. There may be some other secrets behind the other relics we have, too. So..." He paused for a moment, stalwart. "I'm thinking about going to the demon realms myself to investigate! At my next work break, I think I'll go back there."

A few moments of silence ensued.

"You haven't been back yet?"

It was Emi who came up with the obvious question.

"Um...?"

"Oh, you haven't? Uh..."

"Wait, so *that's* what you called all of us over for?"

"I thought the Devil King had paid a return visit long ago."

"Huhh?!"

Emi and Suzuno had friends in the audience. Amane, and even Rika, were excitedly nodding at each other.

"Why would we think otherwise? We know you were in close contact with Camio and the Malebranche chieftains. I assumed you visited them back at New Year's."

"Oh... You did?"

This cold reception took the wind completely out of his sails.

"But um, like, I'm the Devil King, right? If I went back to my realm without telling anyone, I figured you'd all assume I was up to something no good, so I didn't think I should go without any warning. That's why I stayed and left things to Ashiya and Urushihara and the Malebranche..."

"Maou... You really thought about us, didn't you?"

"I'm more shocked you assumed I *wasn't* thinking about anything..."

Chiho seemed slightly moved by this, for some reason. Maou, seeing the other side of the coin, felt conflicted all over again.

"But anyway. Back to the point at hand. The whole conflict between Kinanna and Camio has its roots back in the demon realms, and I get the idea that Satanael left something behind wherever Kinanna lives. We've had a pretty easy time recovering the relics so far thanks to you all, so I don't want to screw up the Astral Gem in the end. So... Um..."

Without warning, a car stopped in front of the apartment, a deliveryman from Sasuke Express hopping out of it. "Oh, it's Mr. Fukuyama," whispered Urushihara, recognizing his face at once.

The man stopped once he noticed the crowd in the front yard, eyebrows raised.

"Umm... I have a Jungle delivery for Mr. Maou?"

The combination of Sasuke Express and Jungle pushed all of Ashiya's buttons simultaneously. He glared up the stairs.

"Urushihara... Today of all days...!"

"Huh? No! It wasn't me, man!" Urushihara briskly shook his head. "I didn't buy anything except the headphones!"

"Oh, sorry. That's actually for me, for a change."

"M-my liege? You purchased something off the net?! What could it have possibly been?!"

Ignoring Ashiya, Maou jogged up to the deliveryman, lizard still under one arm. Signing the receipt, he had him leave the package where he was standing. It was rather large.

"My liege...?"

"Yeah, uh, I have all of you here, so I thought, you know, why not? But Kinanna kind of ate up all my time, so you're gonna have to make do with this."

With that, he took a wrapped package out of the box and gave it to Chiho.

"Here you go, Chi."

"Maou! Is this...?"

It was wrapped in Jungle-themed gift paper, leaving its contents a mystery. It was accompanied by an announcement from Maou even more epoch-making than his promise to visit the demon realms.

"Today's White Day, right? I really wanted to repay you with something more unique and fancy, but I ran out of time, and this is all I could get."

"What...?!"

Chiho, Suzuno, and even Emi were astounded. Acieth, meanwhile, looked like a predator inching in for the kill.

"Um, can I open it?"

"Well, sure…"

Chiho, who was ready to start chewing through the wrapper
unless she heard otherwise, opened it. Inside was a small box of
fruit-flavored candy.

"Ahhh! Ah, ah, ahhh!"

Her eyes lit up like a child as she marveled at the box from every
possible angle.

"Th-thank you so much! I—I can't believe you got me this…!"

"You've done a lot for me, Chi. I had to repay you *today*, at least,
'specially because there aren't any events like this for a while to
come. Sorry I lazed out and bought your gift online, but…"

"I'm so happy, Maou! I almost want to frame this and put it on the
wall!"

"Um, you should probably eat it instead," snickered Maou as he
took more packages out of the box.

"Hey. Rika Suzuki."

"Huh? Me?! Isn't that, like, a ton bigger than Chiho's?!"

Maou presented Rika a box that—in terms of cubic area, at
least—looked a good ten times larger than Chiho's.

"You're special. I factored in what you gave to Ashiya and Urushihara, too."

""Ah…""

Ashiya and Urushihara both groaned. Ashiya, of course, was in
no environment to be thinking about White Day gifts, while Urushihara didn't have anywhere near the thoughtfulness to buy any.

"It *looks* big, but it's light, so don't expect too much. It's some ket-
tle corn from that trendy American place."

"W-well, thank you," Rika said as she accepted the box, unsure
how to react to the regret the other two exhibited. "I mean, I didn't
think I was gonna get anything at all!"

"Next, Suzuno and Acieth."

"I… I thank you. I am surprised…but thank you."

"Woo-hoo! Maou, he remember the White Day! Not believable! Woo-hoo!"

Suzuno awkwardly took her box, while Acieth ripped hers out of Maou's hands and started chowing down, not bothering to hear what it was.

"...You really thought I was that thoughtless all the time, huh? And this is for our landlord and Amane."

"Oh, good heavens, you really shouldn't have!"

Amane blinked. "Huh? Us too? Did we give you anything?"

"You've both helped us out a lot, so. Also... Hey! Alas Ramus!"

"Hiii!"

Alas Ramus toddled up to him, all smiles. She knew an imminent gift from Maou when she saw one.

"Alas Ramus," the beaming Maou said, "today is called White Day. Remember when you gave Daddy chocolate a few weeks ago? Well, today's the day Daddy gives you candy in return. Here you go."

She accepted the box—and when she undid the wrapper, she found the same fruit candy Chiho received. She waved at her, grinning.

"It's the same! So much!!"

"Ah," Suzuno remarked, "hence the fruit candy."

The colorful candy on the package must have reminded him of the Sephirah colors. It made enough sense to her.

Maou scratched his head. "I really had, like, no time, so I wasn't able to choose these very carefully... Oh, also, Emi?"

"...What?"

If this was about White Day, she wasn't involved. She could tell now that, despite expectations, Maou liked this living situation enough to want to preserve it. That was more than enough for her. But having her name called out made her face go blank.

"Here's yours."

"...Buh?"

It wasn't the most intelligent thing, coming out of her lips. But it was all she could manage.

"But I... I didn't give you..."

She really *did* give him chocolate—mixing it in with the huge pile Maou received, unbeknownst to him. There was no way Maou could've found out about it.

"No, you did."

"Huh?!"

Had he noticed?! Emi's face began to burn red, a cold sweat running down it.

If he knew she had given him a bit of chocolate out of duty on the sly, that alone would be enough to die of embarrassment—but if he revealed that in front of all her acquaintances, especially Chiho, it'd be even worse.

"Are—are you sure you have the right person...?"

"How would I confuse *that* for anyone else's?"

"Huh? Wh-what?!"

Maou seemed completely sure he had received chocolate from his nemesis. He must have noticed, somehow. It was time for Emi to face facts.

"Like, no matter how simple it was, there's no way Alas Ramus could make her own chocolate treats without any help."

"Ah......... Ah, yeah!"

She caught herself before she said *Now I get it!* out loud. Yes, she had supervised Alas Ramus's "handmade" chocolate back when Chiho was guiding the demons through the process. *That* was what Maou meant.

"Besides, you really *have* been helping me lately. So this is for that."

"...Thank you."

Neither Chiho nor Suzuno nor Rika seemed to find this exchange suspicious. It relieved Emi, although she was surprised to feel a little disappointed, in a way. Did she *want* Maou to notice the chocolate she gave him?

"Plus, with me getting rejected for that job, I thought you were worrying too much about me in different ways from Chi, so... You

know, I wanted to prove with my actions that you shouldn't freak out about me."

"..."

She had no defense. She had been filled with anxiety about Maou's future. But now, even when she thought she had him all figured out, every one of her predictions turned out wrong; all that worry for nothing.

Why does the Devil King understand what I'm thinking about so well? Why can't I understand what he's thinking? Why do I hate that so much? And why did I want the Devil King to notice my...?

"Oh, also, Emi..."

"Y-yes?!" she replied, standing back at attention.

"Not that I'm bribing you with this or anything, but when I go to the demon realms, I want you to join me."

"Wh-what do you mean?"

"It's not *that* much of a surprise, is it? I'm gonna take Kinanna along, so I want at least one person who can wield holy energy with me, or I'll be stuck if things really go down the toilet. But Suzuno's busy wrangling everyone on Ente Isla, and I can't really take Chi with me over there. So can you help me out when you're not working?"

"But... Me?"

The Devil King, her mortal enemy, was inviting her to come visit his homeland. Emi's eyes burst open, surprised.

"Please! You're the only one I can ask! If you say no, I'm gonna have to turn to Laila, but that's a terrible idea. It'd be huge for me if you came along."

"Huge? That much?"

"That's just mean, Satan! Also, did *I* get any candy?"

Maou and Emi both glared at Laila, whining over to the side.

"What were you expecting?" Maou snipped. "If you want a gift on White Day, ask your husband."

"Maybe I will! Hmph!"

Emi looked up, only to find Maou too busy berating her mother to pay attention to her. The sight of Laila's defiance filled her mind with fatigue.

"It's all right. I have some ready for her."

And the sight of her doting father living up to Maou's expectations made her ten times more fatigued, if that were possible.

"Aw, that's so nice, Yusa! I wish *I* could go to the demon realms," a jealous Chiho said. "I want to see where you were born!"

"I would not recommend it," snickered Ashiya. "It is quite dangerous, for one, and I am not sure there is much a young human girl could do for recreation."

"I also have an interest in life over there," chimed in Suzuno. "If I can find the free time, I would be glad to accompany you…"

"Dude, anyone can go. I'm tired."

"Shut up, Urushihara. Suzuno, if you aren't too busy for it, then great. I just need a holy-magic user, is—"

"A-all right!" Emi reflexively shouted, as if cutting off Maou's near invite. "I'll go, I'll go. It's not gonna take *that* long, is it?"

"Oh, really? You will? Sweet! One day is all I need, okay? We're just gonna search around where Camio met Kinanna."

"W-well, if we're gonna do that, we should go on a day when neither of us have shifts the next day! If we get in an angel fight or something keeps us from coming back to Japan, we'd be in big trouble!"

"Of course. We both have next weekend off, right? Let's do it Saturday."

"S-Saturday? All right. B-but this is my first time going there, so get me whatever I'll need in advance, all right? And Alas Ramus will be along for the ride, so don't forget about her!"

She realized she was speaking more quickly than usual. But she couldn't stop. Why did she cut Maou off before he could formally invite Suzuno to join her? Emi, no longer sure if she really understood herself, followed Maou's instructions and volunteered to join him—and Chiho and Rika were already whispering among themselves about it.

"Chiho, you better have Maou treat you to a really fancy parfait or something next time."

"It's all right… He has a point. I can live with the miracle he gave me today."

"But you know…they're planning a date right in front of you, Chiho! One where they're assuming they'll spend the night together!"

"Chiho! Rika! I can hear you!"

"Oops!"

"Aw, but…"

"What do you mean, a date?"

"You don't have to ask! Look, are we done talking?! Then I'm leaving! See you later! Let's go, Alas Ramus!"

Maou blankly watched the irate, reddened Emi take Alas Ramus away, then turned around.

"…Did I say something wrong?"

"Maou," a scowling Amane said next to her, "as a grown woman, let me give a young guy like you some advice. There's a time and a place for everything, okay? And watch your choice of words. There's a good and a bad way to say everything, depending on the atmosphere. I think I'm starting to understand why you didn't get that job."

"Wh-what's *that* mean?!"

Maou was shocked at this criticism out of nowhere. But everyone else in the front yard silently agreed with her.

THE
DEVIL KING
AND THE
HERO STORM
THE DEMON
REALMS

A red sky above red earth dominated a landscape dotted with black clouds. The wind rushing above them shook the air like a howling giant, offering no solace to anything between heaven and earth. The first sight of the demon realms, the home of Maou and every other demon, took Emi's breath away. It was desolation, dreariness, and sorrow symbolized.

"So this," she managed to whisper, "is the demon—"

"Maou! The sand, it goes in my eyes!!"

"Yeah, it'll do that..."

"<Satan! Why are we in the Greatstone Waste? We will make a fine target for Legoon out here!>"

"Peep-peep! Where's peep-peep?"

"I tell you, I am *not* 'peep-peep'!"

She never finished her whisper.

"..."

Her former mortal enemy had invited her to his homeland—a complicated situation that made for some complex emotions she didn't know what to do with. But her companions were being far too annoying for her to even start on that self-exploratory quest.

"Come on, Alas Ramus. Put on your goggles and mask. You'll get sand in your eyes."

"Maou! My eyes, they hurt! And my mouth, it is full of the sand!"

"I got a set for you, too. Don't tell me you forgot them!"

"This not fair! My big sister, she gets it, but me, no! Give me some! Gimme, gimme, gimme!"

"Stop acting like a begging child! Laila, put them on her!"

"All right, all right. Come here a moment, Acieth."

"Boooo! Maou is a big loser! No good! Mom, what do you have on your head?"

"I have long hair, so I put it up in this scarf to keep as much sand out of it as I could."

"Daddy! Peep-peep! Peep-peep is gone!"

"Peep-peep's right here, Alas Ramus."

"Huh? …No! That's not peep-peep! Scary!"

"Camio, stop making Alas Ramus cry."

"Er, no, um, I am not peep-peep, but I also *am*, in a way…"

"…"

They were loud, and none of them gave Emi's feelings any consideration.

On White Day, Emi had agreed to go with Maou to the demon realms, barely even waiting for him to supply a reason. It turned out he had a number of pretty serious motivations for inviting her and the rest of this party.

First, they needed at least one person stronger at wielding holy magic than Camio, just in case Kinanna's violent spells didn't stop in the demon realms.

Second, with Camael's next move unclear, there was a non-zero chance they'd have to deal with assassins from heaven, and they wanted a bit more firepower on their side than just Maou and Camio. With Acieth on hand, Maou certainly had the muscle to dispatch three angels at the same time—but he still lacked much experience controlling Acieth's force, and the exact nature of this power was still largely a mystery. Better, he thought, to have more stable firepower on hand instead of relying on an unknown like that. The "non-demonic, non-holy power" he busted out against Camael at Sasahata North High School, and the similar force he tapped against

Gabriel and two other assailants in Heavensky, were still question marks.

Third, as Maou had said, if the Devil King went back to his realm, and the humans involved with the assault on heaven found out, knowing the Hero Emilia was accompanying him would put a lot of people's minds at ease.

Fourth, the whole reason they were back here was to jog Kinanna's memory and learn more details about the historical Devil Overlord Satan's relics. Thus, both Kinanna and Camio, who had fought over the Astral Gem, needed to come along.

Fifth, Laila had memories of the Devil Overlord as well as the assorted things that happened in heaven long ago. If they came into contact with an angel, or some of Satanael's past belongings, she might be able to help out.

As a result of all these considerations, the Devil King's first return to his realm since he set off to invade Ente Isla had evolved into what resembled a family vacation.

Alas Ramus, next to her, was whining about the lack of peep-peep since she didn't realize Camio, back in his original form, was that black chicken from before. He tried his best with her, crouching his large body and trying to assuage her anxieties, while Acieth just sat there and let Laila put on her anti-sandstorm equipment for her—two grown-ups attempting to coddle the young ones at the same time. Kinanna, slithering around at their feet, played the role of the pet they couldn't find anyone to take care of at home.

"Ugh..."

Looking back, she had nothing to be nervous about. Certainly, all demons were still the enemy to many Ente Islans, their realm a brutish landscape crawling with them. But by this point, to Emi, the Devil King was nothing but...

"You doing okay, Emi?"

She lifted her head. There, much higher up than usual, a familiar face stared down at her—framed by a single horn on one side of his head and a gigantic body covered in his Devil King's cloak, one that Emi once attempted to pierce through with her sword.

"Let me know if you start feeling sick. This has to be a terrible environment for you."

The grim, foreboding face of the Devil King, leader of demons and nemesis to all humankind, was concerned for Emi. She wondered how he interpreted her sighing.

Yes, the demon realms were pulsing with demonic energy, thick enough that Shiba's warnings of exhausting the supply seemed silly. If a normal human came here, it'd be like sitting in a room full of lethal gas.

"…I'm fine for now, thanks."

The Emi of today meekly accepted the kindness of Satan, a demon no longer her adversary.

"But if it really gets dangerous, I'll transform somewhere Kinanna can't see me."

"All right. But don't push yourself. I've never brought a human to the demon realms before, so I can't say what's gonna happen."

"…Yeah."

If Emi wanted to run at full performance in a demonic force–laden environment that was like a poisonous miasma to most humans, transforming into Hero mode would do much to reduce the strain on her body. But Kinanna had named Legoon the warrior, an angel from heaven, as his arch-nemesis. If the Hero Emilia came along, having a lot of the same external traits as Gabriel and Camael, they didn't know how he'd react. Thus, except for real emergencies, Emi needed to keep that locked away.

"But how come Kinanna's still a lizard if you and Camio are back to your demon forms?"

"Oh, right…"

"Ugh. Use your head a little."

Only now did Satan notice that the pint-sized lizard at their feet hadn't absorbed any demonic energy. He was the exact size he was back at Villa Rosa Sasazuka—where the creature hungrily ate up even the tiniest bit of demonic force Maou released and used it to enlarge himself. Surrounded by all *this*, you'd expect him to be the size of a giant monster out of a movie.

"<Now, Camuinica...>"

As Maou wondered about this, Kinanna looked up at Camio.

"Hmm?"

"<What happened to the Nothung?>"

"...That again?"

This discouraged Maou. In the lizard's senile mind, the Nothung must've been something he had some major regrets about. He hoped a change of scenery to something familiar would change his tune a little, but all he wanted to talk about was that sword.

Camio, likely feeling the same way, looked down at him. Then, at Satan, he said, "...Pardon me, my liege."

"Hmm? What are...? *Ngh?!*"

Suddenly, Camio tapped on Satan's broken horn, injecting his own demonic force into it.

"Owww! What's that for?!"

The pain of having an old wound energized with foreign energy like that brought tears to Satan's eyes.

"One moment, my liege," Camio said, lowering his head. "I just wondered if this could trick him for a period of time."

"Huh? Trick him?"

"Hey, I sense some demonic force coming our way."

Laila pointed toward the eastern sky.

"Hmm?"

Looking that way, they picked up on it—a sort of strong, dark energy flying toward them.

"I will call for it. Excuse me."

Camio flew up and away.

"Huh? Daddy?"

Watching Camio go, Alas Ramus—for reasons only she knew—called the force that had Camio's attention Daddy.

"Is that a sword?"

It was—and Camio had just caught it in midair.

"Is that...?"

It was a familiar blade to Emi and Satan, its scabbard covered in tons of jewels, every inch of it bursting with energy. It was a demon sword, crafted from the Devil King's own horn—and perhaps because the Yesod fragment was taken off the sheath, it was bursting with energy even with the blade not visible.

"Ohhh… That's my…"

"Indeed, it is. This sword is made from fragments of your shattered horn, my liege."

It must have been attracted to the magical force of the Devil King, whose energy it was imbued with. But handling it here in the demon realms, it exhibited an ominous, foreboding strength, far more powerful than when they had last seen it in Choshi.

"So it comes flying to me if I poke at my scar? What kind of curse is that?"

Emi grinned as she looked up at Satan's missing horn. "It's already pretty cursed as it is. Not that it's for me to ask…but you can't fix that thing?"

"Probably not. It got used to make this sword. If I could fashion *that* back into a horn, I could've restored Room 201 to normal, too."

"Your Demonic Highness, I apologize. It was taken at great risk from Ente Isla's Devil's Castle, as a relic from the Devil King we thought we lost…"

Satan shook his head. "It's fine, it's fine. It's not like it won't ever go back to normal."

"Huh?"

"Oh?"

"Here, look. I noticed this the last time I transformed back."

He crouched, giving Emi and Camio a closer examination at the sliced-off stump. When it first happened, the surface was level and flat, like a trunk sawn off a tree—but now, it rose a little bit, forming a small hill.

"It's starting to grow a bit again."

"Is…? Is that how it works?"

"Ah, yes, the shape of your horns *did* change quite drastically as they grew. When you were younger, my liege, they were no longer than one of my claws."

"Right? So yeah, I guess so. Of course, this is after two years of growth, so who knows when they'll both be in balance again."

Satan flicked his other horn.

"Besides, I don't really see a need to get this fixed. It's kind of a symbol of the mistakes I made. If someone cuts your horn off, that hurts in more way than one, and even if you can take the pain, it still sucks. Learning that in time for this war against heaven was good for me. I know to watch out for that." He stood up and smiled at Emi. "Because we've fought enough by now, right? And if, after all this, I'm dumb enough to go back to our old relationship, I'd rather we both just died."

"…!" Emi, not expecting this, was speechless. She blushed. "Wha? That-that-that's not something you can… I—I didn't, like…"

Whether he intended it or not, it was just like what she whined at Chiho about. It made her almost incoherent, for some reason. Satan—Maou—was thinking the same things as her. Emi no longer wanted to fight him, and he no longer wanted to fight her. If they could avoid it, they would.

"I…"

"Ha-ha! Well, let's help out Alas Ramus's family first. Hey, Camio, where was Kinanna's lair again? We can't stay here too long. Camael might still be around, and I'd like to keep other demons from realizing I'm back home for now."

"…"

Camio glanced at Emi quickly. He did not speak to her.

"It is in the direction your demon sword came from, my liege. But if we venture inside unprepared, I fear it'll attract the wrath of Kinanna again. His strength is truly something to be feared, so… Kinanna! Look at this."

"<Hmm?>"

"It is the Nothung."

"Huh? Uh, shouldn't we have taken the real one along?"

Was he trying to make the lizard confuse Satan's demon sword with the Nothung? The real one was still in Ente Isla, and Satan wondered if it was worth the time to bring it over. But before he could suggest it:

"<What is this?!>"

Oh, great, Satan thought.

"<Camuinica! You've abandoned the Nothung until it's deteriorated into *this* sorry state? If I told you once, I told you a thousand times—no matter how long the fight drags on, you must always sharpen it regularly! How will you ever slay Legoon with this?!>"

"Huh?"

Kinanna was angry, all right—but for different reasons than Maou expected.

"<Come here, Camuinica, you inexperienced young fool! I'll sharpen you up right alongside the Nothung! Here we go!>"

The transformation came quite suddenly. Just as Camio went from a black chicken to a proud Pájaro Danino general, the lizard Kinanna's form morphed into a two-legged, muscle-bound warrior in the blink of an eye. The stone they thought was the Astral Gem was embedded in his throat, the dazzling color pattern around his neck shining shades of red in the crimson sky. Taking the demon sword in hand, he extended insect-like wings, also in an array of rainbow colors, and floated into the air.

"<What are you doing, Camuinica?! Join me!>"

Camio placidly nodded. "Yes... Shall we, my liege? And you, too?" Then he flew up, encouraging the others to join him.

Satan half froze for a moment, unsure what to make of this chiseled demon, not at all the reptilian monster he saw in Yoyogi Park. Emi pushed him forward.

"See? Bringing him back here is giving us results. Let's go."

Picking up Alas Ramus, he flew behind Camio.

"A-all right..."

Satan followed along, still unsure.

"What is the matter, Mom?" Acieth asked Laila.

"Oh, um, I just feel like I don't really have anything to contribute, so..."

Satanael, also known as the Devil Overlord Satan, left a set of relics, crystallized pieces of his memory, in the demon realms for reasons only he knew. Laila knew no details about any of them, and she couldn't get anything useful about them out of Gabriel. What was going on while she was denouncing Ignora as mistaken and wandering across realms?

"But, Mom, if you were not there, then Maou, maybe he not be alive? It is fine! You are no useless bum!"

"Acieth, I know you're trying to make me feel better, but I'm not *that* bad off... Maybe you're right, though."

The largest, boldest dreams in the world will lose out every time to a single committed act. These two superpowers, teaming up to stop Ignora—if Laila wasn't around, they wouldn't be here at all.

"Thank you. Now, let's go."

"Okay! Oh, but do not get the cocky, okay, Mom? Suzuno, she say 'Oh, be careful when Laila is raring to go!'"

"...Does she really doubt me that much?"

Maybe it was time for Laila to reconsider her life a little bit. The thought depressed her as she soared into the red sky.

East of Greatstone Waste was a mountainous area that used to be the stronghold of Alciel's Iron Scorpion clan, although it was mostly deserted now. Beyond it lay Kinanna's homeland.

"There it is, my liege."

Camio pointed to the mouth of a large gorge, a crack in what was otherwise a flat patch of land. As if on cue, Kinanna descended, plunging straight inside.

"His comrades won't attack us the moment we go down, will they?"

"No, they won't. That land..."

Camio lowered his voice.

"...is a valley of death."

The bottom of the gorge was not exposed to the howling winds above. In its place was stagnant air and low temperatures. The wind brushing against the top echoed across the canyon like a low rumble, applying pressure to the ears. It was a deep valley, pockmarked with tunnels on the walls that resembled the hives of gigantic demon insects. Around them, toward the top, the wind blew coldly, like the dead of winter.

"You okay, Alas Ramus? Would you be better inside Mommy?"

Emi had no idea what climate to expect, so she and the two Yesod fragments in the group were in warmer clothes. Now, they could all see their breath. Emi hugged Alas Ramus tight, the child hugging her back.

"Mommy, I'm cold."

"I know. Come on in, okay?"

She closed her eyes and fused with Alas Ramus. Away from the cold, Emi could feel a sense of relief wash over her.

"Hey... Maou, I the cold, too, a little..."

"Sure thing. I don't want you poking around here anyway."

"Huh? Ah! I—I did not mean—*hey!!*"

Acieth, hoping for a little sympathy of her own from Maou, instead got sucked into him without any chance to protest. He didn't want her curiosity getting the best of her and driving her down one of those tunnels—but based on her shouting and carrying on in his mind, she must have picked up on that. Maou let it slide. Despite her anger, the cold meant she was in no hurry to go back outside.

Kinanna, the first to touch down, walked along the gorge's bottom and away, not looking back.

"Considering how imposing he is, something seems to be concerning him. Don't get lost, okay? This gorge is full of tunnels."

"As far as he knows, I am Camuinica, and my liege is Satanael. He has memories of spending time with both of them in this land. He must assume we'll follow along without him having to tell us. Don't worry. I have walked this path before. This way."

Camio put his best foot forward, walking with confidence that wiped away Emi's concern. It didn't take long for them to catch up with Kinanna. A few times, he stopped to look around and sniff the air, perhaps wary about something else, then start walking again once he was satisfied.

"Is he keeping an eye out for angels? Or Legoon?"

Camio shook his head at Laila, then pointed at a pile of rubble in a previously unseen corner. "I am not certain myself, but I believe he is as wary of *that* as he is of Legoon."

Upon closer scrutiny, it almost looked like a pile of broken machine parts, an unusual sight to see this far down.

"What's that?"

They had been here for some time, their rusted surfaces hard to tell apart from the boulders that surrounded them, but they still had the straight lines and angles of man-made objects. Emi took a few steps closer, straining to observe them in the dim light.

"Wait, Emi."

Satan put a hand on her shoulder. She turned around, surprised at his insistence, only to find Laila looking at the pile with similar wariness.

"Hey, Camio, that a Silverarm?"

"Likely so."

Another new term. A demon clan, Emi assumed.

"This is a Seraph, a polar patrol battle unit. A bipedal weapon from heaven."

"What?!"

It was something Emi never expected Laila to say...and something she never expected to hear in the demon realms.

"A weapon...? Like, a battle robot?"

"That's right. A pretty old model, but I'm sure of it."

"Stay here, Emi."

"Okay..."

Emi nodded at the stern eyes of Satan, then looked up at his back as he gingerly approached the ruined machine. He was on his home turf, as the Devil King, facing something that was torn to shreds ages ago, but he was still taking every precaution possible.

"The Silverarms," Camio explained to her, "could be called bitter enemies of the Devil King's Army. They were a formidable challenge for both His Demonic Highness and his generals."

As someone who didn't know much about how the Devil King's

Army got its start, Emi could only see those robots as something that must've been really strong at one point.

"It's fully shut down. I don't think its communication systems are online any longer. Camio, do you think Kinanna did this?"

"I would say it is quite likely. Him—or another Lenbrellebelve."

Maou, retreating a little, watched Kinanna as he continued to probe the area, swiveling his head around.

"...How long has he been down here...?"

They walked for perhaps two more hours after reaching the gorge's bottom—and along the way, Satan and his team found several dozen more ruined Silverarms. Why would Silverarms, which once wandered in the area of Satan's Ark south of the Malebranche homeland, wind up all the way down here? They didn't know. Maybe there were even more of them abandoned elsewhere.

Regardless, Kinanna spoke no words to these ruined machines. When he finally stopped, he was in front of a tunnel, one looking little different from the others they saw. The main difference was the large crater in front of it, no doubt created by some powerful force. This crater must have been new—made when Camio encountered Camael, no doubt.

"<Mm? What is this?! Has Legoon's advance guard come here again?!>"

Kinanna, seeming to recognize something was off, quickly ran inside the tunnel.

"Of course," Camio said with a grin as he followed behind, "it was Kinanna who did that, not me or Camael."

The rest of the team continued in, one step back. They quickly found that only the entrance was dark—the rest of the tunnel was not.

"Are those lightbulbs?"

The lights lining the walls were not the luminescent moss or other dim sources of illumination one saw in caves. They appeared to be powered by electricity. What resembled a bare cave up front soon gave way to a paved path, leading to a geometrically designed hallway.

Looking at the walls and floor, Satan's eyes lit up. "Is this...the same material as in Satan's Ark?"

"I did not venture this far in my last visit...but something like this, so far underground?"

Satan and Camio couldn't hide their surprise at the secret space in Kinanna's tunnel. Neither could Laila.

"I... I know this. This is what *we* built. Up in heaven."

She touched one of the walls, looking shocked.

"When he went away from heaven, Satanael took some of the moon's technology with him...but I thought that was only in Satan's Ark. I had no idea there was any of this here... I wonder if Gabriel knows about it."

Satan had already surmised that Satan's Ark was a heavenly creation. But what could Satanael have buried in *this* space, so far away from there? Something so important that he placed Lenbrellebelve guards to protect it?

"Let's hope the answers are on the other side of that door."

A few hundred feet ahead was a door, the design of which nobody on hand had seen before. Kinanna stood in front of it, waiting for them. Nervously swallowing, they approached him.

"<...>"

Once they were all by the door, Kinanna wordlessly turned around, then peered into what looked like a lens on the wall. There were similar devices in Satan's Ark, Satan recalled as the door automatically slid open. He only recognized it as a retinal scanner because he had learned what those were in Japan.

Beyond the door was a small chamber, almost a continuation of the hallway, with the same kind of door on the other end. It didn't seem like a room, and exactly why this small, empty space existed at all was unknown. But nobody sensed any danger, and the party had members strong enough to deal with any surprises at hand. So they entered it, Kinanna taking up position at the next door.

They all stopped, not wanting to rile him. Then the previous door closed behind Emi's back. And just as everyone went on full guard, ready for anything, unexpected things began to happen.

"Whoa?!"

"*Peep?!*"

With a shout, Satan and Camio were engulfed in a dark fog.

"Devil King?! Camio?!"

Emi was about to manifest her holy sword, Laila squaring up for battle herself—but then the fog dissipated, sucked into the walls and ceiling. And what they left behind...

"Hohh, man... What was that all about?"

"*Peep...* That was quite a surprise."

...was Sadao Maou and a black chicken.

"Are you okay?!"

In a panic, Emi ran up to them. Maou, lying on his rear end in shock, didn't appear hurt, apart from the fact that his Devil King cloak was a floppy bedsheet on his human frame.

Camio quickly trundled his small, round body up to Emi.

"It was quite the surprise, but I appear fine... And you?"

"We're all good. Right, Emilia?"

"Yes, I didn't—"

"Huh? Hey, Acieth, you okay?!"

Acieth, fused with Maou, did not fare as well. At once, he released her, only to find a severely nauseated girl, face covered in a cold sweat.

Laila promptly sprinted up to her.

"Acieth?!"

"I... I am okay... Or I want to say...but... It is the tough...*urg*... Maou, that thing, it was good to you...? Your dark force, it was sucked up like vacuum?"

"I dunno... Losing all that force was a surprise, yeah, but I wasn't hurt at all..."

"But you must be..." Acieth winced at the oblivious Maou. "That thing, it takes energy from the core of life... I cannot believe it... Emi and Mom, you are really fine? Maou, Camio, you, too...?"

"Um..."

"Apart from losing that force, yes. Although this could be a *peep* problem..."

Acieth had clearly gone through an ordeal just now, confusing everyone else in the room. Then Emi recalled something that made her shudder.

"Alas Ramus?!"

She materialized as Emi called for her. Her suspicion was right. The child appeared to be unconscious.

"Alas Ramus! Wake up!"

"She's alive, Emilia. Don't worry. She's just unconscious."

Laila stopped Emi before she started trying to shake her awake.

"How can I *not* worry right now?! This came out of nowhere... What's wrong, Alas Ramus? Open your eyes!"

"Calm down, Emilia!"

"...!"

Emi froze at the sound of her mother's scolding. But the energy drained quickly from her body.

"You're her mother! You can't lose your mind at a time like this! Just calm down and prepare for whatever might come next. You know they're far, far stronger than we are. I know you're worried that she's knocked out, but if she's breathing, she's fine. Come on, everyone, look up ahead."

The door before them had opened up at some point. Kinanna was gone, and nothing but darkness greeted them beyond. It seemed to lead to a much larger chamber.

"This room was probably like the air showers you see in factories, so you wouldn't bring demonic energy with you to whatever's coming. It didn't affect Satan or Camio at all, but if this machinery sucks the energy out of people, who knows what's driving it... I never saw anything that did *this* in heaven. If it did that to Acieth and Alas Ramus, I bet we'll find out why up ahead."

"If anything else happens to Alas Ramus, that lizard's going to pay."

Emi fused back with the child, holding her tightly, then wiped the tears from her eyes and peered into the darkness.

"I'm bringing you back, Acieth."

"Okay," she said, still a little pained. "I want the sleep, a little. Unless it is bad, do not wake, okay?"

"All right," Laila declared, "I'll take the leader position from now on. You and Camio can't fight like that; Satan, Emilia, you take the rear."

"Okay."

The four of them went through the second door, all senses finely tuned. Then, as if awaiting their arrival, the large, high-ceilinged chamber lit up.

"What on...?"

Not even Maou, familiar as he was with the state of science and technology in Japan, had seen all the inscrutable, unfathomable machines and devices that filled this room. It looked like a factory, or perhaps a laboratory, with an incredibly high ceiling and a sprawling floor space. On one end was a desk of sorts, equipped with a console and monitors to control the rest of the room. On the other were four capsules on top of platforms, each different sizes and likely meant to house something. One of them, the largest, was bigger than a lot of buildings they had seen; most of the square footage in the room was devoted to this monolithic capsule.

"This...doesn't really match up with my image of Kinanna..."

Emi had a good point. Why would that completely befuddled lizard be connected to heavenly technology, the likes of which not even Laila knew of? He *had* to be involved, given how the retina sensor let him in, but would he sit down at one of these consoles and start controlling all these machines? It was a bit hard to imagine. Ergonomically, the desks and such were clearly made for human-sized operators. Even in his current bipedal form, Kinanna's tail would get in the way.

"So where did he go...?"

"Actually, why didn't he shrink from that mist? He's a demon, too."

"I dunno. But none of this looks like it's running. Let's go see if there's another exit or... Whoa!"

"<What are you going on about, Satan? It has been a while since your last visit. Have you forgotten how to operate this?>"

Just as Maou was checking around the chamber, the capsules began to rumble into motion, Kinanna coming out from behind their platforms.

"<Camuinica, what have you been doing with the Nothung? It's shrunken to the point that you can't even install it in the capsules.>"

"I-install it?"

"<Right. Time to sharpen it.>"

Ignoring the flustered Camio, Kinanna approached a console and began operating it with his clawed fingers, not trying to sit down.

"Oh...?!"

The sword from Satan's horn began to rise.

"Uh, Camio, this is kinda bad, isn't it? Isn't the Nothung supposed to be in that machine? If it's something else, will it break?"

"I—I would think so, but what *peep* can we do about it...?"

"It's starting up!"

Laila, too, couldn't hide her concern about what seemed like impending doom for that machine. But with a low whirring, the demon sword went inside the capsule—and then a fifth rose up from between the other four. It was big enough to house a person, but it was empty, its door open.

"<Right. Oof!>"

"Huh?"

With a measured pace, Kinanna walked inside the capsule, as if he had done it a million times before. It automatically closed, a set of restraints keeping his head in place.

"<Now, time to begin.>"

The restraints were designed to keep the stone buried in his neck exposed. Once they were in place, the entire capsule was cloaked in black mist.

"Demonic force?"

"Could that be the force taken from us? Ah... It is not..."

"No, there's too much of it... Whoa?!"

The concentrated force inside the capsule was clearly even greater than what had just gotten sucked out of the Devil King and his consort.

"*Hrngh...*"

Judging by how Emi, even with her superhuman resistance, was currently retching behind the two of them, there was clearly a fearsome amount of demonic energy being put into that capsule. Its walls didn't let any of it out, but the stench of it alone was affecting the Hero's physical health.

"This...is kind of rough..."

Laila, being an angel, was no exception. She held her hand to her mouth, but her eyes were still focused on Kinanna in his capsule.

"This much force at once... It's enough to suck all the nearby demonic energy out of the atmosphere... Where does it come from...?"

"...!"

Maou remembered: He had seen this happen, long before he had gone to Japan, even before he had united the demon realms. It was in the wastelands to the south, when he was being held prisoner at the Malebranche homeland and sent to defeat the Silverarms running around Satan's Ark.

"No way..."

He had been under the earth's surface then, too. And when he traced his memory that far...

"Hngh?!"

"Devil King?!"

The capsule housing his demon sword began to glow—and the moment it did, Maou collapsed, holding his head against the intense pain.

"Ooowwwwwwwwww!! Wha-what the hell is—? *Aaahhhhh?!*"

"My liege?!"

"S-Satan?! What is it?!"

"Gaaahhhhhh?! My horn... My horrnnnnn?!"

"Hold on, Devil King! Hang in there!"

Emi couldn't be blamed for panicking. A small amount of blood had spouted out of the right side of his head.

"Kinanna! Stop that machine! His Demonic *cheep*... Er, the machine is hurting Satan!"

Camio shouted with unusual volume. It didn't seem to reach Kinanna in the capsule. In fact, the stone in his neck began emitting an even stronger light—and when he absorbed the super-concentrated force inside, he, too, began to shine brightly.

"<Ooohhhhhh...>"

Between his shouting and the whirring of the machine, Kinanna and the demon sword glowed on...and its brightness was directly connected to the pain making Maou writhe around.

"What is this black magic *peep* he's showing us?!"

To anyone else, it would look like Kinanna was inside some elaborate torture device. But it was Maou taking all the pain.

"Agghh! ...Gaaagh!"

"Hang in there, Devil King!"

Emi took out a handkerchief and applied it to Maou's head. It was quickly stained red with his blood.

"Emilia! Keep it held down! ...*Ngh!*"

Laila—a doctor in heaven and a registered nurse in Japan—put her own hand on top of Emi's, applying healing magic to it.

"Nnn...guh...rngh..."

But the blood didn't stop. And while everyone stood around him, helpless, the capsule with the demon sword let out a particularly blinding burst of light.

"Aagh!"

"Devil King!!"

Maou's body spasmed, and then his eyes rolled back. Emi managed to keep him from falling straight to the floor, but Maou was completely unconscious.

"Devil King! Devil King, are you okay? Keep it together!"

He didn't wake up.

"The blood stopped...but..."

It was no doubt because the sword inside the machine was sharpened, as Kinanna would put it. But they had no idea why something that hadn't been part of him for years would affect him this way.

"Oh! Acieth! Is Acieth okay?!"

"I don't know. I can't treat her from the outside. I can't say what's happening to her while he's unconscious..."

"You have Alas Ramus and me here! It shouldn't matter whether he's knocked out or not! Acieth? Can you hear me? Can you get out of there?!"

Emi tried calling for her. There was no response from her or Maou.

"<So did that sharpen it?>"

Then, completely ignorant of the scene outside, Kinanna sluggishly exited his capsule.

"<Kinanna!>" Camio shouted. "<What did you do to that sword? What do you mean by sharpening it?!>"

Kinanna didn't seem to hear him. Instead, he trudged to the other capsule.

"<Don't tell me, Camuinica, you've stopped sharpening it for so long that you've forgotten?>"

Emi had no idea there was such a thing as a lizard's smile until that moment.

"<It means concentrating my life energy within the Astral Gem Satan placed in my body and using it to reenergize the sword.>"

"<!!>"

"Did he just say Astral Gem...?"

"Assuming my Idea Link picked that up correctly..."

Emi and Laila glanced at each other while Camio, at a loss for words, stared at the sword. At first glance, it didn't look any different. As a chicken, he was watching Kinanna from a pretty low angle—but as if Camio was standing there in his usual form, Kinanna brought the sword forward...and let it go in midair.

"*Peep?!*"

With a heavy clunk, the sword landed right in front of Camio's face. Gingerly, he examined it. Its demonic force had been sucked dry in the previous chamber. The scabbard had become discolored and the jewels scraped off of it, perhaps by the light in the capsule.

"Mmph... What...*peep* is this...?"

The sword, while infused with Satan's horn, was otherwise the same as any other metal sword. But Camio felt repelled by it. The aura it emitted made it all but impossible to approach.

"Camio? What is it?"

"Can—can you *peep* pick up the sword for me, Angel? With my current body…"

"Oh? Oh, all right. I hope the machine didn't break it or anything…but at least we know that's really the Astral Gem in his throat, huh?"

Keeping an eye squarely on Kinanna, Laila approached the sword.

"Based on what we just saw, I think it's pretty obvious…"

'Yeah… You're right."

Laila and Emi looked at each other with a mixture of emotions. It was safe to say they knew where the Astral Gem was now. And based on the capsule sizes and Kinanna's Nothung obsession, it seemed clear this very chamber was deeply related to the four relics. And if Kinanna was a sort of "living relic" charged with sharpening the others, it was clear what the other three capsules were for. The capsule he had just put Maou's horn-based demon sword in belonged to the Nothung. The gigantic one near it must've been meant for the Spear of Adramelechinus…

"…Wait."

But then Emi noticed something strange. There were four capsules—one for each relic, she assumed. But Kinanna—i.e., the Astral Gem—went into the central capsule that appeared when the sharpening process began. That made for one too many capsules.

The Sorcery of the False Gold had to go into one of them. One was smaller than the Nothung space; the other a bit larger than that. Emi had never seen the Sorcery tome before, but either way, she couldn't guess what was meant to fill the blank space.

"We aren't still…missing something, are we?"

"Emilia? What is it?"

Laila, not picking up on this, grabbed the demon sword.

"<You need to keep the Nothung sharpened, you know. If you don't do a thorough job of it, you will never neutralize Legoon the warrior.>"

Kinanna was not focused on Laila, despite her being right there with the sword. Perhaps Laila and Emi never even registered in his mind.

"<Now, Satan, it is time for you to slay Legoon once more.>"

This encouragement was lobbed at a prone, unconscious Maou. Emi had enough. Flinging caution to the wind, she glared at Kinanna.

"<Mm...>"

But he still didn't look at her. His face was hardened, sharpened, and it was pointed at neither Emi, nor Laila, nor Maou, nor Camio.

"...Huh?"

"What?"

"What *cheep* is it...?"

Emi, Laila, and Camio followed his gaze. And there...

"Wha?"

"Uh..."

"Ah..."

"<Legoon!!!>"

As the trio stood dumbfounded, the lizard darted among them at lightning speed.

"Agh!"

"Whoa!"

"*Peeeeeep?!*"

A shock wave coursed through the chamber, blowing away the lightweight Camio. Laila withstood it, Emi bracing herself as she held Maou's body, but neither could move while in its grasp.

Since when was that figure there? It was small, a measure smaller than Laila or Emi, and somewhere amid all this fracas, it had taken up residence at the entrance. Kinanna, noticing it, went on the attack with fists raised, but a barrier of golden light was between them, keeping him safely away.

"That's..."

The sight was familiar to Emi. Not the figure, so much as what it was wearing, maybe? She didn't know. But it was clear this was the enemy.

The jet-black, bowl-like visor. The somewhat puffy full-body suit. It was that astronaut—the one who'd appeared aloft in Heavensky, capital of Efzahan, and tried to suck everything with holy energy upward to it.

"…"

"<Nnnnnnngh!!>"

The barrier of light did little to dissuade Kinanna. He bashed against it with his full force, attempting to break through.

"!"

It was hard to tell since the visor was completely opaque, but it seemed like the astronaut flinched back a bit. The stone in Kinanna's throat glowed—and suddenly, his arm punched its way through the wall.

The claws reached the astronaut's helmet, hitting it with a dull thud. Emi thought it might shatter the visor—but Kinanna only managed to push the astronaut's head back a little, causing no damage at all.

"<How did you find this place?!>"

The lizard hammered another fist down at astonishing speed. The astronaut, unable to dodge in time, took the blow head-on. Another dull thud. The suit wasn't damaged.

"…!"

Kinanna, flustered at being so ineffective, flinched for a moment. That was all the astronaut needed. A thickly gloved right hand reached for his throat.

"<Ghn… Kaaahhhh!!>"

"!"

Not trying to undo the grip, Kinanna opened his mouth wide and screamed, his throat releasing sparkling trails of demonic force—a move they'd seen in Yoyogi Park. The astronaut took them at point-blank range, and while her outfit remained undamaged, the figure unhanded him and stepped away.

"<Impressive.>"

Not lunging in for another attack, Kinanna growled at the foe. Or perhaps he couldn't attack at all. Unbelievably, after all that force, he fell to his knees. There were still indentations around his neck where he was choked. Black mist flowed out from them—and bit by bit, he began to shrink.

"<Camuinica! What are you doing? Take the Nothung! Push Legoon back!>"

She didn't understand him, but Emi heard "Camuinica" among the gibberish. It made her click her tongue.

"Peeeeep..."

Camio, bereft of force, couldn't even beat a normal human by this point. And being blown against the wall just now didn't do him any favors. The peeping seemed even more pathetic than usual.

Realizing her back was against the wall, Emi manifested her holy sword.

"Laila, take care of the Devil King!"

"Huh? W-wait, Emilia, you can't right now..."

"This is exactly why I came here! Please!"

"No, Emilia! That's...!!"

Laila's shouting couldn't stop her daughter.

"You don't need to tell me who it is!" She leaped forward, surpassing even Kinanna's speed. "It's Ignora, isn't it?! If I beat her, this ends now!!"

It could only be her. There was no one else who'd attempt to fetch the angels Maou defeated in Heavensky, who made strange advances upon Alas Ramus and Acieth while in the bodies of their respective hosts—and who now fought with Kinanna, a lizard capable of beating Camael at his strongest. In that bulky outfit, no less. The root cause of everything tormenting Emi and her daughter—Ignora, head of heaven.

"Prepare yourself!"

With extreme hostility, Emi instantly transformed—no time to worry about Kinanna's reaction. Turning her holy sword's force up to the strongest level, she smashed it down upon her foe's visor.

But:

"...!"

"No...!!"

Like a father deflecting a sword made by his child out of newspaper, the astronaut globe grabbed the Better Half's blade, stopping it like there was no power—holy or otherwise—behind it. It forced Emi to land awkwardly on the ground, her momentum stunted.

"Y-you're kidding... Why...?"

The sword didn't move. No matter how much she pulled or pushed, the glove kept it frozen in the air. The space suit seemed bereft of energy, but not even Emi's concerted effort could make it budge.

"Emilia! Get away! Put your sword back!!"

"I would if I could!" Emi shouted back at Laila. "But she's...! What're you doing?!"

"Emilia?!"

"My sword! It's coming... No! Stop it, Alas Ramus!!"

With a scream, Emi was blown aside. In front of her was a golden barrier of light, the same that stopped Kinanna's fist. It had sent Emi flying like a bug.

"Agh!!"

"Emilia!!"

Sent helplessly to the floor, Emi's hair and eyes went back to their usual colors, and then she fell unconscious.

"..."

The Better Half was nevertheless in the space suit's hand—still manifested, despite being away from Emi. Twisting her arm, the astronaut took it by the handle, giving it a few test swipes like it belonged to her.

"I-Ignora... Are you Ignora...?"

Laila furtively called her by name. The former comrade that she once respected but turned away from after a difference in opinion. But the astronaut called Ignora did not respond. She didn't even turn her way.

"..."

Wordlessly, she caressed the Yesod fragment ensconced on the handle—and then something unbelievable happened.

"Alas Ramus!!"

Laila's voice was a high-pitched scream now.

The holy sword disappeared, as if melting into the air. All that remained was Alas Ramus in the astronaut's arms, sleeping with a discontented expression.

"Stop! Ignora! That girl…!!"

In a panic, Laila tossed Maou aside and lunged at Ignora, not even bothering to remove the scabbard on the demon sword she carried. But she was no trained fighter, and to the astronaut, it barely even registered as an attack. There was no golden wall. None was required.

The visor turned her way.

"…!!"

That was all it took to stop Laila. She wasn't even four feet away, but she just couldn't extend her arm out to her. Her body erupted in a cold sweat, her legs started to quiver, and she wound up dropping the demon sword.

"…I-Ignora… You…"

"*Laila.*"

From behind the visor, there was a voice she should never have been able to hear.

"*Thank you for helping me.*"

"…What?"

"*Farewell, then.*"

A glove came up to Laila's face, emitting a blinding golden light.

But just then:

"<This is not over yet!!>"

With a cry, the astronaut's wrist was launched upward.

"Ngh!"

"Ahhhh?!"

Kinanna picked up the sword Laila dropped, removing the sheath, and struck the astronaut's arm. The space suit, impervious even to the Better Half at maximum strength, was deflected away by a demon sword that was drained of demonic force a moment ago.

The strike triggered another shock wave of energy, strong enough

to virtually take Laila's head off. The wave smashed the largest capsule and blew a hole in the wall.

"<Nrraaahhhh!!>"

"!!"

For the first time, the astronaut took evasive action. Until now, she
had blocked every attack with either that golden barrier or her own
space suit—but now she was running from a simple steel sword.

"<I will let you take no more of the children of the great tree!
Legoon, prepare to die!>"

Paying no attention to the demonic force bleeding out of his neck,
Kinanna skillfully avoided Alas Ramus as she surged toward the
astronaut. The tip finally reached the visor, the same one that was
undamaged after a direct slash from the Better Half—carving a
small, gold-colored scratch on it.

Then, out of nowhere, Alas Ramus woke up in her arms.

"...Malkuth...?"

The astronaut paused for a moment. Kinanna didn't miss a beat.

"<Keeeeeeeehhhhhhhhhh!!>"

"Wah!"

With a feral scream, he extended his slippery tongue and wrapped
it around Alas Ramus.

"!"

But the astronaut quickly recovered, lunging for the tongue faster
than Laila could see.

"<Ngh!>"

"Wehh-ehhhhh?"

The tongue was a lot sturdier than at first glance. A burst of golden
energy must have come out of the gloves again. There was blood in
the air. Alas Ramus, wrapped around the tip, was shaken violently.

"Ah!"

"<Mngh!>"

"Aaah!!"

Weakened to the point that he couldn't bring enough power to his
attack, Kinanna dropped Alas Ramus. The astronaut reached out,
ready to grab her.

"Hraaaaaaaaaaaaaaaaaaaaaaaah!!"

The scream stopped everyone in their tracks. Acieth Alla had appeared out of nowhere—and the next thing they all knew, her right knee was buried in the chin of the astronaut's visor.

The high-speed surprise attack had a clear effect. But Acieth's assault didn't end there. She landed a whiplike kick on the astronaut's right side, still off-balance and wide open. Nothing Kinanna or Emi did could make her do more than waver a bit, but now she was down on the ground.

"Wah!"

Just then, Alas Ramus, who had fallen to the floor near Acieth, blinked and looked around the chamber. She then realized her clothing was soaked by Kinanna's saliva. "All wet," she sadly proclaimed.

Acieth smiled a little bit at that before firming up her face and handing her over to Laila.

"Mom, take care of Big Sis for me. You can do that, yes?"

"A-Acieth... You..."

Ignoring the dazed angel, Acieth immediately pressed upon the astronaut, still trying to get up. Her foe raised a palm, perhaps trying to counterattack, but Acieth landed another kick on her arm, giving her no time to come to her feet. Raising her leg high, she smashed her heel upon the visor with full force. Her opponent, who seemed so invincible before Emi and Kinanna, was now practically groveling to her.

"You! How dare you do the mean thing to my sister, you turd! How dare you!!"

This sounded like Acieth but with more intensity than even her usual self. And as she spoke, she kept on kicking, virtually tormenting the astronaut—and with each kick, her enemy was sent to the ground again.

"You say something to me! Your head, I will break it! Come on!"

Then she grabbed the astronaut by the neck with one hand, like picking up a tree branch, and used her free hand to land a flurry of body blows on her side.

"…"

Laila just stood there, unable to do anything else. She had nothing to fend off the astronaut with—but somehow, Acieth made it a completely one-sided battle. She wasn't ripping or tearing the space suit itself, but the shock of the blows must've been making it inside, because she was making occasional moves to block her strikes. But given the headlock the astronaut was currently in, there wasn't much she could do. Laila thought about stopping Acieth—but doubted she could, and besides, even if she did, what next?

"What's wrong with Asseth…?"

Alas Ramus looked a bit alarmed at her younger sister's transformation. But she didn't stop. Even Kinanna just stood there, sword in hand, unable to parse this development.

"You! All of you!!"

"A-Acieth…"

Laila's weak voice made it nowhere near Acieth's pounding fists of fury.

"After all…you did to us…!"

"Asseth… No… Don't…"

"Wh-what is it, Alas Ramus…?"

The child squirmed in Laila's arms.

"If only you were never here!!"

"Huh?"

"<Mngh!>"

As Laila and Kinanna watched, an aura of red rose up over the rage-driven Acieth. It lasted for just a moment—but that was all it took.

"…!"

"!!"

The astronaut, totally defenseless before, escaped Acieth's grip the moment the aura blipped in and out of existence. She ran for the exit, but Acieth quickly recovered and came after her. Turning back, she found her assailant's eyes emitting a dull light, resembling but not exactly like the Hero Emilia's scarlet eyes—a light shared by the Yesod fragment glowing on her forehead.

"W-wait, Aci..."

"<No! Not like that!>"

It was Kinanna who moved first. His actions made it look like he was trying to stop Acieth, advancing upon the astronaut as she fled into the corridor beyond.

"Aghh?!"

But the moment she left the atmosphere in the chamber, she let out a scream of pain. The astronaut, realizing this, stopped for just a moment to turn around.

"Don't...go..."

She was faced with murderous red eyes of Acieth glaring at her, even as their glow was starting to fade. She got the hint. In another moment, she was gone.

"Asseth!"

Alas Ramus jumped out of Laila's arms and ran up to Acieth, Laila a beat behind to make sure the astronaut didn't come back for a second round.

"Acieth, are you okay? What happened?!"

"Asseth! Hang in there!"

"Uggh...dammit... I almost had her...Big Sis..."

"What? Asseth! What?!"

"You're all wet... So gross..."

"Nh?"

"Phewwww..."

"Acieth?!"

With that, Acieth closed her eyes and stopped moving. Worried, Laila knelt down by her side but then rolled her eyes as Acieth began to snore deafeningly. She turned to the door; the astronaut appeared to be gone for good. She ran out to the gorge, just in case. There was no sign of any life.

"SKRRRNNNNNN..."

"Asseth! Wake up! Are you okeh? Wake up!"

"<...>"

Returning inside, Laila found Acieth prone. Making an ear-bursting racket, Alas Ramus was slapping her cheek in a futile attempt to wake her up, and Kinanna was just standing there, bleeding from his mouth and emitting black mist from his throat. Maou, Emi, and Camio were down for the count as well, showing no signs of waking up anytime soon. The danger was gone, she could safely say, but Laila still put her head in her hands.

"What is going *on*...?"

✳

"What?!"

At the base of Devil's Castle in the Central Continent, the blood in Suzuno's head began to drain as she heard the hard-to-believe report from Emeralda.

"Are...? Are you sure of that?!"

Emeralda looked similarly strained. "I am indeeeeed," she replied, speaking notably faster than usual. "It happened right after you returned to Japaaan the other day. We received news that Archbishop Robertio, eldest of the Six Archbishops, had died, and it put Sankt Ignoreido, the Sanctuary, and every cathedral worldwide in a tiiizzy."

"Archbishop Robertio..."

The Six Archbishops, the highest decision-making body in the Church, stood at the top of the religion's worldwide bureaucracy; Olba Meiyer used to enjoy a seat among them. There were officially no ranks between Archbishops, but Robertio Igua Valentia was generally seen as having the most influence. No one had served as Archbishop for as long, and even in his advanced age, he was robustly healthy. He did not serve on the front lines against the Devil King's Army, like Olba did, but nonetheless, there were no warning signs that he would die so suddenly. Suzuno thought of a few scenarios—assassination, internal strife, even Olba escaping imprisonment in Saint Aile—but Emeralda dissuaded her against any of those theories.

"Canon Robertio is officially 'taken by a miiiracle.' The other four Archbishops all gave the same tessstimony."

"A miracle? That is what the others said?"

With Robertio, mediator among the group of six, dead, and Olba, a bureaucrat with worldwide influence, no longer among them, the four remaining Archbishops would normally engage in a power struggle to secure their own futures. Whenever someone this high-up died, even from clear natural causes or illness, the death would usually not be announced publicly for some time to come—time needed to work out how to break the news, when to do it, and who'd be appointed in their place. There was no way all four surviving Archbishops would call the cause of his death a miracle.

"Wh-what kind of miracle was this? This was an Archbishop. Are you saying even Archbishop Cervantes said the same thing?"

Cervantes Reberiz, the youngest Archbishop in history, had an equally youthful lust for power. Following Robertio and Olba, he was the de facto third in command among the group. With numbers one and two gone, Cervantes had the perfect chance to seize authority for himself—but instead, he was working in harmony with the other three.

"Wellll…" Emeralda turned pale. "Each of the four says they had the same dreeeam. A dream where Canon Robertio was accepted into heaaaven."

"A dream? In *these* times? What would they use holy dreams like that for?"

There was nothing more annoying to a Church bureaucrat than a king's or a cleric's holy dream. These dreams were usually interpreted as missives or prophecies from God, often in a way that gave the dreamer free rein to engage in all sorts of atrocities. But the situation was beyond even what Suzuno imagined. Emeralda paused for a moment, frowning at the thought.

"In the dream, the 'aaangel' who came to Archbishop Robertio apparently warned of a 'daaanger facing the world.'"

"…!"

The four surviving Archbishops may have all drunk from the abyss of good and evil, each one parched for power and greedy enough to do anything for it—but they were still clerics and believers. Suzuno

turned white as a sheet of paper. Now, she could imagine the absolute worst-case scenario, one that went well beyond her imagination.

"N-no... No!!"

To many practitioners who believed in the Church faith in Ente
Isla, the Six Archbishops ranked above even the king of their own
nation in most cases. They were literally as lofty as you could get,
and their words held sway just as massive as prophecies from God.
Their powers were so vast that, at times of peace, they would deliberately stage political differences among themselves, so as not to
turn public opinion or axes of conflict too far in one direction. If all
four of these "prophets" were saying the same thing, that would be
accepted by the people as the truth, without question.

"The angel in the dream said this: 'Another evil is gathering
anew, in the center of the world. All good people, it is time to come
together, rise up, and slay this evil.'"

"It cannot be... After everything was going so well..."

Suzuno felt her knees tremble. She could no longer even pretend
to hold her composure. This was too much.

"Our 'enemy' must have aimed for this moment. Choosing
the worst possible method at the best possible time with the least
amount of work to crush our objective."

"What about General Rumack...?"

"General Rumack needs to attend to her own nation. She is already
on her way home. I obtained this information ahead of all the other
nations because I was able to place one of my staff in our capital's
grand cathedral, to make up for the inquisition against me. But I
fear it will not be enough of a time advantage to leverage before the
news begins to spread."

*We should have considered this from the start. Why did we assume
the enemy would be so foolishly honest that they'd gladly stage a fron-
tal attack against us?*

The enemy, in this case, was the gods of the planet. It'd be easy
for them to interfere with Suzuno and sow chaos around the
world. One of the angels in heaven must have killed Robertio, then
stood in the surviving Archbishops' dreams, inciting them in the

name of their kind. All so they could crush Suzuno's plan without exposing themselves to any danger. And if the four Archbishops all act under the same volition, there would be no way in this world to stop them.

"Do you think Saint Aile and the Western Island would comply?"

"We can't think of this as a time of peace anymore. It would depend on what action Rumack chooses to take, but that fiend Pippin and his accursed band are still latched on to her, festering like black mold with their Church connections. I would not be too optimistic. And even if Saint Aile does not comply..."

As a Church leader, Suzuno didn't need to be told, but Emeralda did anyway.

"The combined forces of the Sankt Ignoreido headquarters, the Sanctuaries, and the Church knight corps dotted around the world would be approximately equal to Efzahan's combined armies."

"Damn...them...!!"

Suzuno balled her hands into fists tight enough to draw blood.

"Why are the Devil King and Emilia not here yet?! Please... Please come back! If this keeps up..."

Her pained shouting, imbued with her deep pessimism for the future, reached no listener.

"If this keeps up, we will shed blood that needs no shedding!"

– To be continued –

THE AUTHOR, THE AFTERWORD, AND YOU!

Sorry to keep you waiting. Yes, I'm aware.

It's been eleven months since Volume 16 of *The Devil Is a Part-Timer!* For what basically feels like a year, progress on the main story has ground to a halt. Volume 0-II, which came out between Volumes 16 and 17 in Japan, is naturally an indispensable part of building the *Devil* world setting, but a prequel is a prequel nonetheless.

So what have I been doing the past eleven months? As I think many of you know, I've written two new books—*Diego no Kyojin* and *Yusha no Segare*—as well as *The Devil Is a Part Timer! High School N!*, a self-written spin-off. Thanks to that, I've received some passionate support in the past year, along the lines of "You must spend every second writing *Devil*," "No snacks until you write another *Devil* volume," and "Ah, Wagahara! Just one more before I die!"

This series has now spanned six years and seventeen official main volumes. My stock of dreams, the things I thought—"Boy, it'd sure be nice if I could write about this or that if this keeps up"—back when I started, has finally run dry. In order to stay fresh in my storytelling, whether with *Devil* or anything else, I needed to regain my thought process for building a story from scratch. But that's my own issue, of course, so either way, I apologize for making you wait.

To make up for that (kind of), a new drama CD for *The Devil Is a Part-Timer!* is coming out in June 2017 in Japan, right after this volume's release! It features the cast from the anime, of course, as well as a certain character who isn't in the anime at all! Yes! Finally! I hope you'll check it out!

As long as I've been doing this, I've made you wait quite a bit this time, but thanks to that, we have a fair amount more to offer. And as long as the people in this story have been engaged with it, they're still living every day unfazed by the grind, thinking of the future, and appreciating everyone they're with. I hope you'll see them again in the next volume—and elsewhere as well.

Until then!

THE DEVIL KING SCREWS UP BUYING A TIE

Note: This is an original, previously unpublished story, not included in the Japanese print version of The Devil Is a Part Timer!, *Vol. 17.*

Inside the Devil's Castle that towered over Ente Isla's Central Continent, Maou sat on his throne, surveying the selection spread out on the tatami-mat floor before him.

"So here's what I've got."

Meanwhile, Chiho and Rika, the couple being shown this spread, gave each other worried looks.

"Um…"

"Maou, the suit you have… You bought it a long time ago, right? With Ashiya?"

"Yeah. Did he tell you?"

"Uh, yeah, kinda. So uh, did you buy *this* back then, too?"

She pointed at one of the items, arms folded.

"No, I bought that new a bit ago."

Hearing this, Rika brought a hand to her temple, shaking her head in exasperation.

"Why did you pick a pea-green paisley tie?"

"Is…? Is that bad?'

"It's gross. Awful."

The blow made Maou flinch on his throne. Seeing Chiho wistfully nod her agreement with a guilty expression in his peripheral vision only added to the shock.

On the tatami mats was the business suit Maou would wear for his managerial training. It featured a charcoal-gray top and bottom, a white button-down shirt, a black belt, leather boots, and a tie. The tie Maou had picked out for himself was being singled out for punishment.

"You'd have to be kind of a pudgier middle-aged guy for this to work on you."

Maou was unable to counter this brutal follow-up attack. Chiho, feeling sorry for him, decided to send out a lifeboat.

"B-but if you actually put it on, maybe it'll feel different! You chose that for yourself, so just try it on."

"Yeah, good point. Can you turn away from me for a bit?"

They did, giving the depressed Devil King time to start changing. But Rika still looked down in the dumps.

"Okay, I'm ready."

"Yep. Nope."

Two words provided all the finisher Rika needed to slay him. Chiho, so surprised by what she saw, couldn't even respond.

"You didn't tie it right, which I'll ignore for now, but it doesn't match the rest of your outfit. At all."

"...Okay."

All Chiho could do was smile awkwardly. "I mean," she ventured, "your suit's cut to be neat and slender, but the colors on the tie alone make you balloon up. It stands out too much. Plus, there's pink in the paisley pattern, and between that and the pea green, it doesn't look very wintry, which is...you know..."

"Complex, intricate patterns, especially in bright colors, are hard to match. Like Chiho suggested, if you're totally married to this tie, then save it for spring. If you pair it with a lighter-colored piece of outerwear, I can see that working, but this isn't the kind of tie you wear to job training in midwinter."

"R-really? I bought it because I liked it, but..."

They felt bad for Maou as he loosened his tie. But he was applying for full-time managerial work. It was a job hunt, basically, and if he couldn't look the part in his dress, he'd stand out in a detrimental way. That was why Rika and Chiho hardened their hearts a little to give their unfiltered advice...

"Okay, so how about this one?"

...but the next tie he broke out left them at a loss for words.

It had a large embroidered coat of arms on it, with equal measures of black, yellow, and red—just like the flag of Germany. To get away with wearing this, you'd have to be either a student in an elite boarding school or a German Olympic athlete.

"...Chiho, Chiho, is it me or does the Devil King have a serious lack of fashion sense?"

"I—I don't think he's so bad most of the time... When we went out before, he dressed pretty simply, but it was still flattering..."

Chiho recalled what Maou wore on their Shinjuku date, before she'd met Emi.

"Oh, really? I've only ever seen him in sweats or MgRonald uniforms."

"...You know, apart from one particular day, same here."

"Hey, I don't know what you girls are whispering over there, but I can tell it's nothing good about me."

Maou had had enough of watching the backs of their heads as they gossiped in hushed tones about him. Then Emi stuck her head in.

"Rika, Chiho, Bell made some tea. Do you want any? ...Is that what you're wearing to training, Devil King? You should try another tie. It doesn't look right on you at all."

With that short review, she walked off—leaving the utterly defeated Devil King slumped on his throne, bested by the Hero's unexpected finisher.

"Hey, uh, cheer up."

"Um, you know, I could help you go out and pick something else..."

They were honestly starting to sympathize with the poor guy. But then a swirl of light appeared next to Maou—and in the blink of an eye, it took the form of Shirou Ashiya.

"Welcome back, Ashiya!"

He had spent most of his time in Ente Isla lately, but judging by the plastic bag in his hand, he was back from his first shopping trip to Japan in a while.

"Ah, hello to you two. Were you helping my liege with his clothing for his managerial training?"

He walked past the dazed Maou, taking two rectangular boxes out from his bag and placing them on the tatami space.

"Your Demonic Highness, I just happen to have these for you."

"Ashiya, are those…?"

"They are ties, my liege."

""Pfft!""

Chiho and Rika both snorted.

"I had a suspicion that your selections from before would be a bit too adventurous for a training or interview situation. I apologize if I am being too nosy, but I made some selections of my own, based on your suit and shirt."

One was a wine-red tie, reserved and with no pattern. The other was a relaxed silver-and-red stripe. Both would pair perfectly with Maou's suit.

"Red ties work well in winter, and I hear that, when expressing your views to another person, it lends a stronger impression to your words. The colors on the striped tie are a tad heavy, but the design is refined enough to work in summer as well. I hope you will give them a try."

"" … ""

That was when it finally dawned on Chiho. That dated wardrobe from Shinjuku—*here* is who lurked behind it.

"Chiho?"

"Y-yes?"

"I'm gonna be rooting for ya, you know, but it's gonna be hard to beat that 'mother-in-law' he's got."

Chiho crouched, feeling a tad dizzy.

"I—I still have my hands full learning how to sew…"

Maou, meanwhile, just eyed the new ties, too weakened to move.

"Man, it's sure great to have friends who're honest with you…"

It was on the warm side in the Central Continent, but Ashiya's earnest helpfulness—and the girls' overly honest feedback—made a cold, dry wind blow over his heart. Back on Earth, it was early January...and Maou's managerial training was about to turn a new corner.

COMBATANTS WILL BE DISPATCHED!